Evernight Publishing

www.evernightpublishing.com

NASH

DEDICATION

I want to say a big thank you to my editor, Karyn White.
Without her Nash wouldn't be the story that it is. She is
amazing and is always willing to help me improve my
craft, thank you.

Also, a huge thank you to my readers. You're all
wonderful and I hope you fall in love with Nash like I
did.

NASH

NASH

The Skulls, 3

Sam Crescent

Copyright © 2014

Prologue

Snitch sat back in the warehouse he'd taken control of watching his men screw the whore they'd found on the city streets. The owner of the warehouse was dead at his feet surrounded in a puddle of blood. The little fucking weasel had been trying to fob him off with the Darkness accounts. He ran the club that moved from city to city, partying and doing whatever the fuck he wanted to do.

Throwing his cigarette onto the body, he gave the deceased another firm kick to the ribs. The only plan the little shit could come up with was Fort Wills. The Darkness, his motorcycle group, was running on fumes. The drugs were being delivered outside of Fort Wills, and no one wanted to touch him or his crew. Fucking Tiny. That bastard, the leader of The Skulls, had been a thorn in his side for as long as he could remember. Snitch let out some more steam, kicking the fucker on the floor while also imagining it was Tiny's body. Fort Wills had been taken from him many years ago, and he'd been biding his time to get it back. Then this little shit had been trying to make out he didn't know what Snitch and the boys needed. Darkness had every intention of getting the fucking town back but not until the right moment.

"The dude is dead," Battle said, sitting beside him. The other man's trousers were unbuttoned.

"The whore any good?" Snitch asked.

"No. She's dry as fucking shit." Battle tipped his beer back, taking a long drink.

"When are the others going to get here?" Snitch wasn't interested in the whore anymore. The last twenty years he'd been waiting to get his town back, and he was so close he could taste it.

"Scars has everything we need, and the other boys are doing their stuff. You shouldn't have killed Rupert there. He was a good way to get into Fort Wills." Battle pointed at the dead body.

"I don't care what he was offering me. Telling me I should take Fort Wills was the final straw." He spat back at the body, hating the effect Rupert had on him.

"I'm just saying this is no way to keep a low profile. You're so close to getting what you want, boss." Battle sounded a little too serious for Snitch's liking.

"Do you doubt me?"

"No."

"This is going to work. Rupert was a loose end. We're going to get what we always wanted, and then you'll be laughing at this moment." Snitch lit up another cigarette and checked the clock. The sounds of moaning were driving him crazy. He wasn't in the mood for fucking. The only thing he wanted was the shit to bring The Skulls down and take over the town he had once owned.

Thirty minutes later Scars and several of his other men were walking in. They were dressed in regular jeans, their hair shaved off, but they wore pussy caps. No one would have suspected the men were part of a biker club.

"What you got?" Snitch asked, standing up.

"Gold." Scars was the one who answered. "Get rid of her."

The woman was gone within minutes, and the light was trained on the table. All the beer bottles and cigarettes were on the floor from Snitch swiping his hand across the table.

"This is the layout of the town." Scars showed the layouts with the pictures he'd taken. Everything was clear, and Snitch found himself remembering the good old days of his time in the small town. Then his memories went back to Tiny, and the anger was back. He would use anything to take on the town.

"The cops leave them alone. They're nothing more than civilians with badges. They do fuck all." Scars pointed at the men, none of whom Snitch recognized. "Their security is weak. They've been rebuilding everything since the druggies tried to take over."

Scars explained everything Snitch already knew. The damage that had been done to The Skulls was legendary. Most of the biker groups within the vicinity had heard about it.

"Moving on from the town and shit. They're still tight, and all of them are together." Scars started to put photographs on the table. "Tiny is the leader as we all know. Getting to him is not going to work, especially with Alex in the mix with them all." Snitch saw the Vegas casino owner, and his anger turned to outright rage. With each name spoken Scars put down a photograph to associate with the name. "Lash, Nash, Murphy, Butch, Zero, Blaine, and Steven are the closest we could find. They're the key to getting Tiny. Then we've got their women. Angel is married to Lash. Tate,

Tiny's daughter, is with Murphy." Snitch snorted. He could only imagine how Tiny took that. "Eva is the other woman who is in Tiny's life. I don't know how she is connected to Tiny, but there is a connection. Then we've got the surrounding women, Kelsey, Sophia, and Sandy. There are more women, but these seem to be the ones of importance. Then you've got the three leftover Lions who are on the outskirts. I don't think they're really trusted."

"I've got a question," Kite said. He was a younger member and only interested in pussy and dope.

"What?" Snitch asked, annoyed with the interruption.

"Why do we think we're going to work when another group, The Lions, tried to overthrow Tiny and failed, and then the druggies tried and fucking failed? The Skulls are untouchable."

In the next breath, Snitch put his fist in Kite's face, shutting him up.

Pointing at the picture of the women, Snitch started to speak up. "The Skulls' weakness is their women. We hit them where they least expect it."

"We take out their women?" Scars asked.

"Yeah, we take out their women. Also, we're not going to go in all guns blazing. We've got a plan. The Lions and the druggies went in without a plan. They tried take over. No one can take over from The Skulls unless you take them down one by one."

"What about Chaos Bleeds? Tiny will call for them," Battle said, mentioning the only other motorcycle club who was close to Tiny.

"They won't be a problem. They're nowhere near us. Last I heard they were tracking down a whore," Snitch said. He always kept an eye on the surrounding clubs.

"I also looked into the other thing you asked," Scars said, producing a couple of pictures. "These men will be the perfect front to do what we need."

Snitch stared at the pictures of murderers, rapists, and other criminals. "Do you think they'll work for us?"

"They'll work for money and a chance to get away from the system," Scars said. "They're what we need."

"Contact them, tell these fuckers the score." Snitch tapped the picture with the name "Gill" on top. All of the men in the pictures looked vicious. If they caused a problem for him Snitch would end them.

"They follow your orders?" Scars asked.

"They follow my orders. No one dies until I know what is going on. I'm the one in charge." Slamming his fist down on the table, Snitch felt the stirrings of arousal. He was going to get his town back, and Tiny was going to get what was coming to him.

NASH

Chapter One

Nash stared up at the ceiling, but he couldn't see a thing in front of him. Everything was blurry as the coke he'd just inhaled went straight to his brain. Kate's supply, which he'd found within her belongings that Sophia had given him, hadn't lasted long. The shit he'd found by beating one of the local drug dealers in the next town over was sending him in a spin. Fuck, if he didn't get his shit together, Tiny was going to out him. The club had few rules, but one of the few rules was no drugs. They transported the shit, but they never took the stuff. He lay on his bed, his mind going a mile a minute and his body bursting with energy. The high was always so addictive, and he loved it.

Running a hand down his face, he couldn't stop giggling. The drugs were the most fun he'd experienced in years. Not even being balls deep in pussy could compare to the rush of being high. His thoughts turned to Sophia, the one woman he could never have.

Go back to her. Don't take no for an answer.

Even as the thoughts entered his mind, Nash cut them off. He wasn't going to be some kind of fucking pussy by chasing a bitch. Forcing himself to forget about her, he brought himself 'round to the high he was currently experiencing. To think he'd missed out on all this shit by staying in control to follow in his father's and brother's footsteps. The Skulls had been his life for as long as he could remember. There was nothing else he wanted to do with his life other than be a Skull. However, he wanted Sophia and could no longer have her because of the fucking drugs. At least that was one of the reasons he couldn't claim Sophia. *Fuck!* All the problems were crashing down on him, threatening to crush him. Nothing was going to spoil his high. No wonder Kate loved drugs. He saw the attraction.

Not that he was addicted.

Laughing, Nash let his hand fall to the floor. He hung off the bottom of his bed staring at everything oddly. Thinking about Kate brought back memories of Sophia, no matter how many times he tried to forget about her, and his rush came crashing down around him. The one woman he wanted more than anything and he couldn't have her because of his relationship with her whore of her sister.

"Correction, dead whore," he said. Speaking to himself had become a pastime to him. No one would listen to him, and he tried not to spend too much time around the other Skulls. The moment Tiny realized he was using, he'd be out on his ass. "Can't have big brother on my case." The Skulls was the only thing that made sense in his world.

"Are you fucking kidding me?" Lash asked. Turning his head slightly, Nash saw his big brother stood near the open doorway with Angel right behind him. Angel was a blonde and innocent looking type. She reminded him a little of Sophia in the innocent look but not the hair. No, there was nothing blonde about his woman. Sophia was all midnight black hair and deep brown eyes.

His cock thickened thinking about his sweet, innocent Sophia. Not that he could ever have her. It wasn't possible for him to have the woman of his dreams. Nope, he'd fucked her sister instead, while also thinking about Sophia. He was totally fucked, and now he was taking drugs. Nash laughed, thinking about how long it had taken him to fuck his life over.

Fuck, he really needed to get a life.

"What's going on, Lash?" Angel asked. Her voice was sweet. Nash really did love his sister-in-law. She never judged anyone within the club or the women, but she stuck beside his brother. The couple should win some award for the strength and love between them.

"He's fucking high." Lash pulled her into the room, slamming the door behind him.

"High? If he's high then Tiny's going—"

"To kick his ass when he finds out. Nash will be out on his ass for the first time in the world," Lash said, interrupting his woman.

"You've got to help him." Angel was as sweet as her voice. What was it about innocent women that the Skulls liked? Nash was starting to hate all the innocence going on around the clubhouse. They needed to find some kinky women who liked being tied up and spanked. Then he'd have a much better time with everything. Rolling over, he ended up on his ass, laughing. "He's in really bad shape."

Lash grabbed him by the jacket he was wearing. "Fuck, brother. When was the last time you washed?" Lash winced away at the stench coming from Nash.

Nash shrugged as he couldn't remember.

In one swift move, Lash was tugging him toward the bathroom, barking orders at Angel at the same time. He was dumped in the shower and the water turned on. Growling in anger, Nash tried to hit out at his brother, but Lash dodged the blows easily while pulling off Nash's clothes. If he hadn't been high then his brother wouldn't be trying to get him out of his clothes.

Once he was naked, Angel took the soiled clothing away. He was surprised Lash let Angel see him butt ass naked. Last time he checked, his brother was on the possessive side.

"Do you want to be kicked out of the club? Is this your deal?" Lash asked.

The high he'd been having moments ago was crashing all around him. The highs didn't last long all the time. His highs varied from thirty minutes to two hours. The fix was always short, and he never wanted to keep doing it. He'd not been trying to do anything other than deal with his life. Why did his brother have to come and ruin every single moment he had?

"Fuck off," Nash said, closing his eyes. He was trying to escape everything.

What are you trying to escape? Your life is not a problem. Taking drugs is the fucking problem.

His face was gripped tightly. He opened his eyes, seeing Lash looking angry. Nash couldn't recall a time when Lash had been this angry or at least when the anger was directed at him.

"You're not getting away with shit that easily. When did you start fucking using?" Lash asked.

The grip on his face tightened. If Lash wasn't careful he'd break Nash's jaw. Along with Killer, his brother was The Skulls' muscle now. Both men were hard as rocks, and he knew Lash could kill a man with his bare hands.

"I found some stash and needed a pick-me-up. I got it, and now I like it. I don't have a problem." He shoved Lash's arm away, stepping under the cold water.

"You don't have a problem?" Lash asked.

"No, I don't."

Out of the corner of his eye, he saw Lash speak with Angel, then kiss her on the lips before turning back to him. The sound of the bedroom door being slammed echoed through to the bathroom.

"If you don't have a problem then please fucking tell me how a guy from the next town over was found beaten almost to death, but he was able to tell your description."

Nash froze under the water not saying a word. He thought he'd covered his tracks. Looking for drugs in Fort Wills was dangerous and fucking stupid. Tiny knew everything that was going on inside his town. Mess with Tiny and you messed with the whole Skulls. Nash had only wanted a pick-me-up.

"Did I also forget to mention this guy, the one that was beaten, is a known druggie? He supplies and takes the shit. You have put The Skulls back on the map, you shit-head, but not just for distribution, no, you've got us all on the mark for taking the shit as well through the rumor mill." Lash stopped, stepping away. "Alex is going ape shit over this. You've messed up with the next shipment 'cause we've got to lay low. Enemies are created by not meeting bargains, shit-head."

Nash listened to everything Lash said feeling his stomach turn.

Turning off the shower, he ignored his shaking hand. Lash handed him a towel.

"Tiny's on the warpath, and when he comes at you, you better be careful," Lash said.

"You're not going to stop him?"

"No, I'm not. Maybe getting your ass hurt or even kicked out might make you realize the shit going down." Lash looked him up and down.

He was surprised by the look of disgust on Lash's face.

"What?" Nash asked, getting angry.

"I'm just thinking about Mom and Dad. I wonder what they'd have to say to your addiction. The Skulls is not a place to be messing around."

Lash turned to leave. Fisting his hands at his side, Nash stopped himself from asking for help.

He didn't have a problem, and there was no way he was going to let his brother talk him into thinking he had a problem.

At the door Lash turned. He stalked back toward him, and Nash waited.

Nash didn't expect the fist, especially from his brother. He went down as the punch knocked him off balance. His brother hovered over him.

"You ever bring shit like that near my woman again and I'll fucking kill you." Lash turned away, without looking back.

Grabbing the side of his face, Nash tried to get to his feet unsteadily. When he looked at his reflection in the mirror he saw the blood flowing from his lip.

Checking out his appearance he saw how the drugs he'd been taking affected his body. He rarely ate anymore, and the signs of not eating were starting to show. His skin looked pale, and there was an unhealthy sheen to his skin.

Fuck, he looked a mess, nothing like the man he was a couple of months ago.

That's what the drugs do to you.

Nash cut off the thought, brushed his teeth, and grabbed his clothes. He didn't need confirmation in the mirror that he looked like shit because he felt it.

Opening his bedroom door he headed downstairs to get some breakfast. Hardy and Rose were sat at the table. Several of the sweet-butts were cooking, but for the most part the clubhouse was empty.

"Where is everyone?" he asked.

Hardy glared at him, clearing his throat. Rose left immediately and the sweet-butts.

"What the hell's going on?" Nash ran fingers through his long hair, shocked by how much it had grown.

"They're out working. Lash covered for your ass again," Hardy said, standing up.

The respect Nash had for Hardy was high. He hated the look of disgust in the other man's eyes. Nash was shocked by the looks his brother and now Hardy were giving him.

"I don't know what you're talking about."

"No? I know a drug addict when I see one. I don't like you being at the clubhouse, but Tiny's got too many problems with Eva and the club to see your problems. We all see it, and the guys don't like it. We've got women and children who visit here, regularly. Drugs are not part of the deal with us." Hardy folded his hands over his chest, stepping close. "I'm giving you a chance to get clean, or I'm making Tiny aware of the fact." He turned to look in the direction where Rose walked off. "My woman means the world to me. You put her in danger, and I'll end you."

With those parting words, Hardy left. Standing in the empty clubhouse, Nash zeroed in on Mikey's picture. The older biker had been killed four months ago by one of their enemies. It had been that long since the old man had died, but it felt like he'd been gone far longer. Nash missed him. Mikey was the one guy who knew how to handle everything. Tiny was the leader, the guy in charge, but Mikey had been the voice of reason. Nash had been taking drugs for over two months. The fact he hadn't been caught shocked him. Tiny really must be distracted with the rebuild of the club, Tate's wedding, and everything else to do with their lives. Nash's luck would run out sooner rather than later. He knew it down to his soul.

Staring at the picture Nash realized he'd been controlled by the drugs longer than he thought. Staring down at his hands, he vowed to get sober from it all. No drinking, no drugs, and no rough partying.

His hands started to shake, and the scent of booze lingered in the air. Drink was never really a problem. He could handle one drink.

****

Sophia Wright stared at the box in front of her. Ever since her landlord had been calling for her rent she'd had no choice but to get another job in the boxing factory. Between her waitressing job and the factory job she was earning enough to make ends meet. Providing nothing happened in her life like illness or, heck, actually having a life, she'd be fine. When she learned that Edward Myers, or Nash as he was known as to most people, had been paying for her place and that he'd stopped paying suddenly, she'd been shocked. She hadn't realized he was paying for her place, and then she'd been hurt. He'd moved her into a place that she couldn't afford, but she loved.

Shaking her head, she got back to business of making up the box in front of her. If she didn't make up her quota her boss was going to be on her ass for more. She hated her boss. He was a fucking asshole.

Without this job I can't live.

She kept saying the same thing over and over again. With everything that happened in her life in the last few months she'd dropped out of college. Her heart wasn't in the studying at all. After she'd quit college, she tossed all of her books in the trash. There was no need for her to try to improve her life. Fort Wills wasn't raving on the job front. The town was controlled by bikers, and that alone made finding work hard. For her it was difficult as Kate, her sister, had portrayed an image that many others believed Sophia to share.

Plenty of women she'd grown up with wanted to be an old lady or a sweet-butt. She didn't want any of it. When Kate, her deceased sister, brought a Skull home, Sophia had been shocked. Edward, or Nash as he was better known, was nothing like the bikers she'd imagined in her mind. He'd been sweet, thoughtful, and the complete opposite of the biker image he portrayed. Whenever they'd been together, he'd been so nice, not once commenting on her plus size figure. In fact, she'd started to wonder what he ever saw in her sister.

"Get your head out of your ass, Sophia. Those boxes won't make themselves," her boss, Willy, said.

Ignoring his comments, she sped up her work.

Need the job. Need the job. Need the job.

It didn't matter how many times she said the words, what she did was boring.

Her boss got right in close behind her. She didn't make a sound and kept working as if he wasn't there. "You need to keep that speed at all times if you want to keep this job."

He threatened the end of her job every day. At first she'd been afraid in case he did take away her work, which was why she put up with his crap. She'd called him out on sexual harassment, and he'd thrown Kate in her face. Who would believe her when everyone knew how Kate was? She didn't know why some people judged her on Kate's actions, but it was a small town, and she knew what that meant. Her life had really gone to shit since her sister's death and her kicking Nash out of her life.

Fight it.

Sophia didn't fight. She dealt with the problem at hand and ignored everything else she could. There was no one else to fight for her. She was all alone in the world.

Taking each unmade box, she made them up and sent them back down the line without question. Glancing up she saw several of the other workers smirking at her. Willy put his hand on her hip, and she tensed up. There was a vibe she got from Willy that made her uneasy. He wasn't a good man. She saw the evil lurking in his eyes, which was so dramatic that it caused her to freak out inside.

"You know, if you were a bit more open to me I could make your workplace a hell of a lot better for you." He whispered the words against her ear.

She gasped, grabbing his hand before he could let it wander. "I'm fine where I am, thank you."

Stepping out of his space, she tried to make the boxes up from an odd angle. Willy kept glaring at her. She knew he'd find a way to make her pay. Today was not going to be that day. He stormed off without saying a word.

Licking her lips she continued working only stopping for lunch when needed. She didn't make friends with anyone at work. She hadn't been at the boxing factory long, and a lot of them didn't like her. Kate had a reputation that spread far wider than Sophia anticipated.

Get over it. Your sister does not control everything.

In her mind's eye, Kate did.

When work was finished she went to the room where her coat and bag were stored. On the way out another man, Gill she thought his name was, stepped in front of her. He reminded her a lot of Willy. The danger he posed terrified her. Chancing a look around the room she noted that no one was around to witness their interaction.

The past couple of weeks she'd been stopped by many people intent on talking with her or to say something horrid about her sister.

"What do you want?" she asked, getting angrier by the second at being forced into a corner.

"What's the rush, babe?" A couple of his friends had stayed behind to smirk.

"Got work to do." Hitching her bag on her shoulder she made to go to the door. Gill stopped her with a hand on her arm.

"I didn't say you could go."

Her heart started to pound. The grip on her arm was too tight. Biting her lip she stared up at another man wanting something she wasn't prepared to give. His gaze wandered down the length of her body.

Seriously? Her body was huge. She enjoyed cooking and eating, and her shape proved that. Kate liked to remind her every day how men hated women with curves.

"Kate was a game girl. She loved to party, and I'm thinking you're the same."

Rolling her arms, Sophia shook her head. "You're wrong. I'm nothing like my sister." She tugged her arm out of his hold, glaring at him.

"You're not being very nice."

"I'm not a nice girl," she said, glaring at him.

"I don't like your attitude." The man before her was stronger than she was. She cried out as he slammed her against the lockers pushing his body against her. "I think it's time you showed me the same attention Kate liked."

His breath was rancid. She cried out as his hand covered her mouth, muffling the noise. No one could hear her, and his other hand was caressing down her body.

As suddenly as he'd trapped her, she was free. What was it about these men? They had come to Fort Wills over a month ago. She saw only them at the factory but never around the town. Did any of The Skulls know them? Sophia cursed her lack of knowledge. She didn't even know what was going on in her own town.

"I believe the lady said no."

There was her answer. The Skulls didn't know them. Sophia looked up hoping to see Edward. His brother, Nigel, was stood in his place. The cut of his leather jacket was showing off The Skulls' emblem clearly. She took a deep breath loving the fact she could relax. The Skulls always made her feel safe.

Then why did you send Edward away?

"We're not looking for trouble," Gill said.

"Good, get out." Nigel let him go, shoving Gill out the door.

"Thank you," she said, gaining Nigel's attention.

He turned to her scowling. "Has Nash been to see you?" he asked.

She shook her head. "I've not seen him in a long time."

Lash took a step closer to her. The man before her was not the man Edward described as his brother. Lash was entirely Skull. His real name left her mind as she stared up at him.

"Something happened between you and my brother."

"Nothing happened." She stared down at her feet. The lie felt bitter on her lips. She'd been a bitch and pushed him away. When he'd walked out of her apartment all those months ago she wished she could take back what she said.

"No? Well my brother is using, so I'm guessing something happened," Lash said.

At his words she looked up. "Drugs? Edward is using drugs?"

"His name is Nash, and yeah, he's using."

"Are you sure?"

"He's off his face all the time. Whatever set him off, you better fix it." Lash rested a hand on the locker beside her head. "I don't know you, and it won't be a problem to me to get rid of you. Fix my brother, or I'll fix you. Do you understand me?"

She nodded, gulping past the panic inside her. Crap, she'd just been threatened, and she'd not seen Nash in so long.

"Good." Lash turned away and walked out.

Leaving the room she headed in the direction of her apartment. She couldn't afford a car, and walking wasn't a problem to her. Keeping her head down she tried to think about everything Lash said.

Don't call them by real names. They're not Edward and Nigel anymore. They're Nash and Lash.

Whenever she thought of Nash she felt an answering pulse between her thighs. He'd been the only man to make her yearn. She'd watched him with Kate and felt jealous of her sister. The guilt swamped her as she recalled the feelings consuming her at her sister's presence and now she was dead. She and Kate had been as different as chalk and cheese. They were not alike at all. They didn't even like the same stuff, but Sophia was attracted to Nash. He was the only person she'd ever felt anything for.

And I pushed him away.

Taking a deep breath, she pulled out her keys and looked up. She paused when she saw Nash leaning against his bike.

This was the first time she'd seen him since sending him away that day. He looked thinner than she remembered, and his locks were dark with grease.

Stepping close, she felt her heart speed up.

"Hello," she said.

Chapter Two

Sophia was more beautiful than he remembered. The sun was shining down on her giving her an air of innocence that took his breath away. Her dark midnight hair was bound together with a band at the back. Glancing down her body he noted the plastic bangles on her wrist. He'd bought her several of those bangles when he realized she liked wearing them. She wore a pair of jeans and a checkered shirt. The leather jacket was a new addition. He'd never seen her in clothes like these before. She looked a little hard around the edges. Her face was clear of any make up.

"Hello, Sophia," he said.

His hands were shaking. He'd taken three shots of whiskey before heading out to see her. Getting a chance to be with her, Nash was debating his decision to drink at all. He also thought Lash had been here minutes before, but he wasn't sure.

"Are you all right?" she asked.

"Yeah, I'm good. I've missed you and wanted to see how you were doing." He'd gone to the college and been unable to find her.

"I'm doing good. You?"

Everything seemed stilted between them. Looking down at the floor he nodded. "I've been great."

He watched as she looked past his shoulder. "It's been too long since I last saw you. I don't like not seeing you."

"You sent me away, Sophia. I'm not the kind of guy who sticks around after being kicked to the curb."

"I know, I'm sorry. I shouldn't have said anything. So, how have you been?"

"Shit has been busy. I went to the college, and you weren't there. Is today a free period or something?" he asked, needing to hear her voice.

She shook her head. "No, I quit."

"What?"

"I don't need college anymore. I'm working to keep my apartment."

Nash frowned. "Keeping your apartment? You don't need to worry about that. I've got it covered."

A mask came over her. Her hands went to her hips. "No, you haven't. I can't believe you started paying for my apartment." She stopped, and he watched her close her eyes.

He'd seen her do it several times while he'd been with Kate. When he'd asked what it was about, Kate told him Sophia had a problem with her anger. Nash didn't believe it. In the years he'd known her, he'd never once seen Kate lose it.

"I don't need your money, Nash. I never did."

When she used his Skull name, he winced. She'd always called him by his given name. "This wasn't about the fucking money, Sophia. I was helping you out."

"Why? You didn't owe me anything. We don't owe each other fuck all. You were with Kate, and now she's dead." She brushed past him, ending their talk.

Leaving his bike, Nash followed her inside the building, refusing to back down even as his stomach turned. Fuck, he could do with a high.

"What the hell are you trying to say?" he asked.

She kept walking up the stairs. He couldn't stop his gaze from wandering to the curves of her ass. Nash wanted to reach out and touch her. He wondered what she'd do if he caressed her tempting body. Doing so would probably get him into a lot of trouble.

Sophia opened the door to her apartment heading inside. She tried to close the door on him, but he wouldn't let her. Nash was stronger than she was, and he used his strength to push his way into her space, determined to get answers.

"Why are you here?" she asked.

"I want answers. I was with Kate, but there was nothing else between us. Kate meant nothing to me."

"So my sister was just a bit of fun for you to have on the side." She pushed some hair off her face, and he saw her cheeks were red.

"Kate knew the score. Besides, she was a first class bitch to you. Kate didn't like you. She sure as shit didn't care about you." He stepped closer, wanting, no needing, to touch her.

"It doesn't matter what was between Kate and me. We were sisters."

"I never cared about Kate."

She shook her head, stepping back. "Why are you here?"

"I came to see you."

"Why?"

Because I can't breathe, and I need to know you're all right.

"We're friends."

"No, you wanted a hell of a lot more than friendship. My sister was gone, and you were moving onto the next girl."

He felt his anger growing with her accusations. "That was not what happened, and you know it," he said, growling.

"It wasn't? You could have fooled me. You kissed me, remember?" Her arms were folded. She'd dropped her bag to the floor.

Nash was speechless by what he was seeing. Sophia had always been quiet, sweet around him. The woman before him was not sweet or light. There was a dark edge to her that he couldn't describe or understand. What had he been missing?

"What's going on with you?" he asked.

"Nothing. You're here trying to get answers. I want you to answer *my* question." Her voice rose, yelling at him.

"I kissed you because I wanted to, Sophia."

"Why? Are you giving the fat girl a pity fuck?" she asked.

The anger spilled out. Grabbing the picture frame from the drawer unit beside him, he threw it across the room. The frame landed against the wall, smashing. Sophia didn't flinch. She looked startled. Her gaze moved from the frame to him.

"Don't ever say shit about yourself like that. I never thought of you in that way, Sophia. I kissed you because I wanted you." He stopped, putting his shaking hands on his hips. "Fine, you want answers, then I'll tell you the truth. "I was fucking your sister so I could be closer to you. I couldn't stand Kate. I was with her for the easy fuck she was. When I wanted to get my dick wet, she was there. Satisfied?" he asked.

Tears were streaming down her face. "Get out."

"No. I was with Kate for you."

"What?"

He laughed. "Shocked you, have I? Guess what, baby? I wanted you. I couldn't give a shit about Kate, and I don't even miss her. I'm sorry she's dead. She was your sister, and I know that's going to be hard to deal with, but I don't give a shit about her being gone or not. You were the one I wanted."

Nash let it all out without leaving anything left between them. She looked a little pale from his outburst. For too long they'd let their situation slide. He wasn't going to let Sophia mistake his feelings again.

"You used my sister to get to me?" He nodded. "Why?"

Taking a step closer, she took a step back. Nash stalked her until she was trapped by the kitchen counter. Putting his hands either side of her on the counter, he leaned in close. "You make me ache, Sophia. When I look at you, I want to make you mine all the time. You're all I can think about. I want you badly."

She licked her lips, staring at him. He moaned.

"Lash came to see me today."

He tensed up. Her words were the last thing he'd expected her to say. "What?"

"Your brother came to see me. He wanted to ask me a couple of questions about you."

Stepping back, Nash felt nervous. He thought he'd seen his brother's bike, but he couldn't be sure.

"What did he want?" he asked.

"To tell me to fix you. You're using drugs, aren't you?"

Shame unlike anything he'd ever felt crawled over him.

"I don't know what you're talking about." He didn't look into her eyes. The moment he gave in and looked into her eyes, it was over.

"Kate died because of those fucking things, and you're using them."

Glancing up, he saw the accusation in her eyes. It was all too much for him.

"You don't know me, and you're not the boss of me."

"Drugs killed Kate. I'm not watching you do the same." She walked past him, opening up the front door. "Get the fuck out. I'm not getting involved with you."

"We're friends."

"You've done fine without me these last few months. I'm sure you can deal with this crap without me."

Nash stared at the open door. Her eyes were downcast.

"What happened to you?" he asked.

"What do you mean?" She looked up finally meeting his eyes.

"You were so sweet and charming."

The tears she'd wiped away began falling once again. "You really don't know me at all."

He frowned, getting closer. "Sophia, please."

"No. I don't want any part in this at all. We're done."

She shoved him out of the door and slammed it closed. He heard the lock turning.

"Sophia, open up," he said. Nash waited for her to say something.

Nothing happened. Slamming his fist against the door, Nash stormed off. He didn't need Sophia, bitch that she was, or his brother the meddling bastard. He didn't need any of them.

Running downstairs, he left the apartment block and climbed onto his bike. He needed a score, and he knew just where to get one. For those few seconds the club, his brother, and even Sophia meant nothing to him.

Gunning his machine, he travelled into the next town going to the worst part of it. Climbing the stairs of the rundown building, he noted the whores and addicts decorating the stairwell. Ignoring them all and the voice in his head telling him to get away, he slammed open the door.

The guy he'd beaten up the other week was sat at the table weighing everything out.

"I want my stuff," Nash said.

"I've been told not to give to you."

Pulling out his weapon, Nash showed off his gun. "Give me my stuff, or I'll shoot your balls off. Your choice." He was done playing games. Nash needed to lose himself before the reality of everything came crashing down all around him.

****

Letting out a breath, Sophia slipped onto the floor waiting for him to leave. When he thumped the door, she jumped but didn't do anything. The sound of his feet down the stairwell made her relax.

"Breathe, Sophia, breathe," she said.

There was nothing else she could do to help Nash. Kate had been high on the drugs toward the later stage of her life, and she wasn't dealing with more drugs.

Turning her gaze toward one of the few photographs she owned of the two of them together, she saw Kate smiling back at her. The Skulls had been amazing when she died. She imagined it was down to Nash, getting the funeral paid for when he didn't have to.

She was broke and wouldn't have given a great service at all. Throughout it all, Nash had been there by her side, holding her hand the whole time. He'd been her rock through the worst time in her life, and she'd kicked him to the curb as if he was trash.

Tears filled her eyes once again, threatening to spill over.

Those few weeks she'd felt like a princess in his company. He'd taken care of everything for once. All of her life she'd been the one responsible for everything. If it wasn't for her, Kate would have made them homeless a time or two. Sophia had gone to college in an attempt to make a better life for the pair of them.

She wondered what Kate would think of her now. Alone, working two jobs, and having kicked out a Skull. Her sister believed in The Skulls and the protection they brought. There was a time when she'd believed in Nash. His taking drugs would start the end of him. Sophia couldn't watch him destroy his life, not another person she cared about dying through fucking drugs.

Pushing her fringe off her face, Sophia saw it was a little after five. She needed to get dressed and ready for her evening to late night shift at the diner.

Getting up from the floor, she headed to the bathroom. After a quick shower she changed into her waitressing uniform and then added a pair of tights to cover her legs. She didn't like showing too much skin off.

Picking her bag up, she headed out making sure to lock her apartment door. She walked the distance to the diner, needing the air to clear her muddled thoughts.

He's not worth it.

No one stopped her to talk or tried to make her feel welcome. Since her sister's death the treatment of the locals had gotten worse, far worse.

Entering the diner she saw several of The Skulls sat at a table. Murphy was one of the men she recognized. He was looking across the diner, and Sophia saw Tate sat with several girlfriends talking.

She'd just kicked a Skull out of her life, and now a bunch of them were at the diner. *Great, just great.*

It was going to be a long night. Entering the back, she hung up her jacket and bag. Jackie, the owner, was talking to herself as she did the crossword puzzle in the paper.

"You're a little early," Jackie said. "I hope you're not wanting to leave early."

"No, I'm good." There was nothing waiting for her when she got home or for her to stay at home.

"Good. With The Skulls here, things could get pretty ugly. Last time they ate in my diner I was closed for six months repairing the damage they made."

"Why don't you just kick them out?"

Jackie burst out laughing. "Honey, you don't kick out the law in this town."

"The Skulls are not the law," Sophia said, muttering the words underneath her breath.

"Might as well be." Jackie heaved out of her chair. "We better get cracking. The other girls are working already. I'm sure you're needed."

Wrapping the apron around her waist Sophia made her way outside. Molly, another of the women who worked at the diner, was shaking her head.

"What?" Sophia asked.

"I'm not serving them. You can serve them. Your sister was buds with them. I'm not having anything to do with them." Molly left her alone.

"Great." Grabbing her pad she made her way toward their table. People stared at her as she walked past. Ignoring stares had become easy to her.

The women or the men? She looked at the two tables and settled on dealing with the women first.

"Sophia, honey, it's been a lifetime," Tate said.

Kelsey, Eva, Sandy, and Angel were sat at the table with Tate. She smiled at all the women.

"What can I get you?" Sophia asked, avoiding the question.

"Are you going to make this difficult for me?" Tate was speaking louder gaining more attention.

Shaking her head, Sophia took a quick look around. Some of the customers were watching them while others were more interested in their own food.

"Not at all. I've got work to do."

"Well we're celebrating. Angel is expecting. This one is going to be great. I can feel it."

She glanced at the beautiful blonde woman, who was blushing a deep red color. The men at the other table whooped.

"Lash is joining us soon. He's dealing with some problems with the club," Angel said. Her voice was so small.

"I can't believe you don't demand to know more about what he's doing," Tate said.

"It's not my business, and I'm happy with what I've got."

Tate blew a raspberry and started to order.

Sophia took down all of their orders and read them back. When she made to move away, Eva grabbed her hand. "How are you, honey? You've not been by the clubhouse."

Sophia felt the emotions welling up inside her.

"Erm, it's nothing. I've been busy. I've not got a lot of free time, and well, Nash doesn't want me there." Sophia thought about before. Then Nash would have wanted her there, but twice she'd pushed him away now. There was no way he would want her at the clubhouse anymore.

"Nonsense. It's not up to Nash what you do or where you go. You're always welcome to the clubhouse as far as I'm concerned."

"I appreciate that." Sophia smiled and pulled her hand, trying to get away from the group of women. They knew too much, and as far as Sophia was concerned, they saw too much.

They all knew she wouldn't be taking up any of their offers. She'd rather be alone than having to deal with the bikers all day every day.

Going to the front of the diner, she put their orders through. As she was handling their order, Lash walked through the door. His gaze landed on her.

Her hands started to shake, and she tried to ignore the sick feeling swamping her.

"Did you do as I asked?" he asked, coming to stand beside her.

She looked behind her to see who was watching them.

"Don't worry about them. I want to know your answer." Lash, clearly, wasn't a very patient man.

"We talked, but nothing happened."

Lash frowned at her. "What went on?"

"Nothing. There is nothing going on between Nash and me."

"There's not?" Lash asked.

She shook her head.

He leaned in close, making her nervous. This man had killed before. All of The Skulls had killed. She'd heard the rumors, and Kate was pretty vocal about everything. Kate had told her that Lash was responsible for killing Angel's dad. There was no way she wanted to be on Lash's bad side. She didn't want to be on his good *or* bad side. Sophia knew he loved his brother and would do everything to protect Nash.

"No, there's not."

"You're wrong. Nash wants you, and he's finding solace in drugs."

"That's not my fault. He was with Kate."

"Kate didn't make him end up on drugs. I've never seen Nash like this. You better make sure he doesn't fuck up," Lash said, moving away. She watched him go to Angel.

Yearning hit her deeply as Lash put on a display. She guessed he wasn't putting on a show for anyone else. The kiss he gave Angel was purely about giving his woman some loving. She wished there was a man out there who would give her the same kind of attention.

Nash would have gladly been the one to give you some loving, and you pushed him away.

Blocking out the thoughts she tried to focus on everything else. When Nash walked into the diner an hour later, she saw the other Skulls tense up. Taking a good look at him from behind the counter, she saw he was a little unsteady on his feet. His eyes were bloodshot, and around his nose was white powder. Shit, she'd never seen him like this. Nash always seemed totally in control to her. Not once in all of the time she'd known him had he ever let something else take charge, but the drugs had really started to.

Some of the locals were shocked but didn't say anything. Lash looked tense. His gaze went to her before settling on his brother.

When Lash mentioned drugs she'd not really believed him at all. At the apartment she'd been blinded by other things Nash was evoking with his presence. Seeing the evidence for herself, she was bewildered. Nash was always in control. She was totally taken back by him being high.

"Come on, big brother, we've got to celebrate," Nash said. His voice was really loud. She watched as he took a beer from inside his jacket and popped the lid off.

Her heart was racing. This was going to end badly. She was sure of it.

Nash turned to face her, the smile on his face disappearing. "Everything is complete now. We've even got Kate's sister to give us some action. I'm sure she's like her sister in many ways." His voice was loud enough for the whole diner to hear his comparison.

Humiliation hit Sophia in ways she wasn't expecting. All the time she'd known Nash he'd never treated her in such a way.

"Let's face it. Kate was a whore."

"Nash!"

Unable to handle the look in his eyes, she walked toward the back of the diner. Jackie followed her.

"Don't listen to him. He's being a little fucker."

"He's comparing me to Kate like everyone does," Sophia said.

"You're nothing like your sister, and you know it. Ignore him. He'll regret this in the morning."

She nodded and went back out. The rest of The Skulls tried to stop him from saying anything to her. There was no shutting Nash up. She took the jibes and kept working. Every once in a while she felt tears were close to the surface.

The women no longer looked happy with what was going on. Tate kept looking at Murphy. When she grabbed their glasses and plates Sophia saw Nash reach out toward her. Nash didn't get chance to put his hands on her as Murphy grabbed the other man tugging him out of the diner. She wasn't going to say anything to them, but she'd never been so thankful for anything before in her life.

Lash glanced at her, but she ducked her head finishing up the cleaning. In no time at all, The Skulls and their women were gone, and she could breathe a sigh of relief.

****

"He's off the rails. I've never seen him like this," Lash said. After everything he'd seen that day he knew it was only a matter of time before Tiny took everything away from Nash.

"What are you doing to do?" Angel asked.

"I don't know." He turned to see her sprawled naked on the bed. His cock thickened, wanting inside her once again. She was pregnant with his son or daughter, and she looked so fucking sexy.

"You can't do everything for your brother. Nash needs to help himself as well."

This was the first time he'd talked to her about the club business. Nash was his brother, but the drug addiction was going to turn into a club problem.

Moving toward the bed, he sat beside her, facing the floor. She wrapped her arms around his neck, kissing him. His cock got harder.

"I know. I'm more afraid of what Tiny will do. He hates drugs, and seeing Nash like this, it's going to cut him up and make him lash out. My brother is crashing into everything Tiny has tried to protect. The drugs stay out of Fort Wills." Lash ran his fingers through his hair, trying to clear his thoughts. They did the drug runs, and Tiny was clear that none of them was to be using.

"You'll handle it."

"Hardy had a word with him as well," Lash said. "If Hardy's seen what's going on then it's only a matter of time before Tiny does."

"Tiny's trying to work stuff out with Eva. He's distracted for now."

Lash shook his head. "He's not. The club will always come first. You know that's the truth."

He blew out a breath wishing there was something more he could do. It was only a matter of time before Tiny found out the truth. Lash only hoped Tiny remembered Nash as a boy, as otherwise his brother was well and truly fucked.

Chapter Three

One week later

Giving up the drugs was not a good idea, and Nash didn't have a problem with them. He was more in control than ever before. Locking his bedroom door, he pulled out his stash of white powder and moved toward the bedroom. Tiny had called in all the members for a meeting, and he had twenty minutes before he was needed.

Going through to his bathroom, Nash locked the door. He pulled out his tray and started to arrange the powder in a line. Rolling up a note, he placed the note toward the powder and inhaled. The buzz happened immediately.

After he'd snorted a couple more lines Nash was more than ready to face downstairs. He ran some water, wetting his hair and wiping away the evidence of what he'd done. Nash felt alive and full of energy. Once he was finished, he pocketed his gun and made his way downstairs. Rose, Tate, Angel, and several of the women were playing cards around a table. The clubhouse was buzzing. Lash was talking with Blaine, and the prospects were waiting for work to be done.

Slamming his palm down on the counter he ordered a beer. The prospect looked unsure about getting him what he wanted. Nash saw the boy was looking toward his brother.

"Hey, fuckwad, don't look toward my brother. I want a beer, and get me a fucking beer."

"Nash, go easy. He's new," Lash said, suddenly standing beside him.

Jerking toward his brother, Nash saw his brother was frowning. "What the fuck are you doing telling the prospect not to get me a drink?"

"Tiny gave the order, no drinks."

"He's never given a shit before. Why is he changing his mind?" Nash asked.

The room had gone silent.

Stop this. This is not like you.

No matter how hard he tried, Nash couldn't stop.

"Stop this, Nash. You're going to make everything worse."

Smiling, Nash looked around, settling on Angel. "Why don't you start worrying about knocking up your slut and leave my drinking to me."

It was the wrong thing to say, and in the back of his mind, Nash couldn't believe what he'd just done.

Lash didn't wait. He hit out, slamming his fist in the side of Nash's face.

"Who the fuck do you think you're talking to?" Lash asked. "That's my woman, Nash. My old lady and you think I'm going to let you disrespect her?"

The other hit made Nash laugh. Getting to his feet he found his gun, and he raised it in the air. Something didn't feel right about him. "Come on, guys, life is a party. We shouldn't be wasting it on bitches or whores or old ladies."

Before he could stop himself, he pulled the trigger. The shot rang out, and what followed was chaos.

Tiny charged out of his office, and Eva was flat on the floor.

"What the fuck is going on here?"

Nash dropped the gun to the floor, and another shot rang out.

"Eva, are you all right?" Lash asked.

"Yeah, I'm fine."

Blaine was getting up from the floor. "I saw where he was pointing. He had a clear headshot of Eva."

"What?" Tate asked. The whole club was tense.

Nash was watching everything as if he wasn't part of the show. It was as if he'd escaped his body and was watching from the outside. Lash was stood with Angel, who'd been thrown to the floor by Steven. Eva was pale, and Tate looked ready to murder him.

"Nash had a clear shot of Eva's head. If I hadn't done what I did, he was going to kill her," Blaine said.

"I wasn't."

Tiny was in front of him in a blink of an eye. "You stupid little fucking shit." The lapels of his jacket were tugged, and he was being dragged outside. The sun blinded him for a second, and he was thrown to the ground. Glancing around him, Nash watched as the other Skulls gathered around him. Even Alex Allen was there doing business and he'd witness Nash's fall. Before all the drugs had taken over, Nash recalled that the other man was trying to move back to Fort Wills.

"I didn't mean to hurt anyone. I was having a little fun," Nash said, giggling. The laughter was uncontrollable. In the back of his mind he knew he'd fucked up and should be begging for forgiveness. Instead he found the whole situation funny.

"Fun? Shooting a firearm in my club and you're calling it fucking fun." Tiny's hands tightened into fists by his side. The danger lurked in front of Nash, and he couldn't give a shit.

"He's not himself," Hardy said. Nash was shocked by the other club member sticking up for him, especially after he'd threatened to out him.

"I see the problem with my own Skull, and I'm not going to stand for it." Tiny stopped everyone from talking. "I gave you a reprieve because of Kate. She

43

wasn't your old lady but a sweet-butt. She meant nothing, and I still gave you time. I've given you too much fucking time, and it stops now." Tiny stared at him with disgust.

The reality of his situation started to wake Nash up.

"It's here, Sir." Turning around, Nash saw one of the prospects holding his bag of white powder. The sight of his habit sent humiliation straight to his core.

"You little shit," Nash said, walking toward the man. He stopped moving, and Tiny held onto him, stopping him from going anywhere.

"What do you think you're doing?" Tiny asked.

"He had no fucking right to go through my shit."

Shut up. You're in the wrong. Shut up.

Lash walked out of the clubhouse with Angel, Tate, and Murphy in tow.

The disappointment on Lash's face brought Nash's whole world crashing down.

"How long have you been protecting him, Lash?" Tiny asked. There was no getting away from what was about to happen. Nash knew the end of his time was coming close.

"He's my brother."

Angel was holding Lash's hand tightly.

I've fucked up.

Nash felt himself wake up completely. Opening his eyes, he remembered what he had done to Sophia a week ago when his brother had been celebrating Angel's pregnancy. He'd gone back to his drug dealer and gotten more of the stuff that had brought about this.

He'd not seen Sophia in a week. The last time he'd seen her he'd been a total bastard to her.

You don't deserve her.

Tiny raised his fist, and the first hit connected with his jaw. Nash went down, covering his face. When he opened his eyes he saw most of The Skulls standing with their arms folded. He'd brought this on himself. Butch, Lash, Hardy, Stink, Zero, Killer, Whizz, and Time were all there, including more of the men he'd been working with since he was patched into The Skulls to witness his end.

Druggie.

Addict.

Quitter.

Asshole.

Dangerous.

All the words rang out through his mind taunting him. Getting to his knees he climbed to his feet.

"You think you can be a drug taking asshole in my club you've got another think coming." Tiny reached out tearing the cut off his back. Nash tried to fight, but it was useless. He was a little boy again only this time the man who had once given him comfort was tearing the comfort away from him by pulling the only thing he'd ever wanted, his leather cut for The Skulls. Tiny had been there for him when his parents were killed.

"Fucking stop it," Nash said, feeling like a child instead of the twenty-nine year old man he actually was.

"You don't deserve this cut." Tiny threw it in the trash, and Nash watched as he lit a match and started to torch his leather jacket.

"Tiny," Lash said.

He looked over toward his brother seeing the pain in Lash's eyes. Nash felt like he was breaking apart inside.

"Stay out of this. I have rules. A couple of rules, Lash, and this fucker has taken the piss out of my rules." Tiny turned back toward him.

Nash had seen Tony let loose on men who caused his family pain. The club was part of that family, and Nash had made the club a laughing stock. His actions put a dark ring around the club and made them look weak to their enemies. Dropping to his knees, Nash hung his head.

"Get to your fucking feet," Tiny said.

No one spoke up, and Nash realized he'd fucked up big time. When he didn't stand up, Tiny grabbed a chunk of his hair and brought him to his feet.

Ever since he'd joined The Skulls, Nash never thought he'd be the one facing this punishment. He'd prided himself on being an integral part of the group. In the last few months he'd fucked up big. Staring in Tiny's eyes, Nash knew he didn't have a choice. Raising his fists, Nash got ready to defend himself.

This was the price of bringing drugs into the group. He was the only one stupid enough to think he could get away with it. Tiny's wrath also had to do with him putting Eva in trouble. Their leader wouldn't claim Eva as his old lady, but everyone knew the truth. Anyone who laid a finger on the woman would end up dead after being tortured first.

Fuck, he'd almost killed her.

Nash blocked the first punch with ease. The next hit came at his ribs then to his stomach. Trying to get a hit of his own in was difficult. Tiny was in the peak of health and the strongest of them all.

Three strikes landed to his face knocking him back. Pain exploded behind his eyes. Tiny wasn't in the mood for playing. This attack was cold, harsh, and if Nash wasn't careful he wouldn't last the next ten minutes. With each hit the leader of The Skulls was getting angrier. The hits were getting harder, and Nash spit blood out onto the tarmac.

"Your father would be fucking ashamed of you," Tiny said. "He was my right hand man. He left you to me, and I helped raise you with Patricia, Eva, and fucking Mikey. You had everything you could want, and you turned into a fucking druggie." Tiny slammed his foot into Nash's stomach.

Going down to the floor, Nash went to his knees coughing and spitting more blood out of his mouth. The pain was intense, and he couldn't hold on any longer. Tiny was on the warpath, and nothing was going to stop it.

You fucked up, Edward.

This had nothing to do with The Skulls. The club was what made him strong. What he'd done today was fuck up in ways he never thought he could.

Accepting the beating, Nash wished for death, finally letting go.

****

"You've got to stop him, Lash," Sandy said. "He's bleeding, and if he takes more blows it will kill him."

"Are you sure?" Lash asked, wincing as another kick landed on his brother. He wanted to stop Tiny, but Nash needed this. The last few months had been a disaster when it came to his brother. There was nothing else Lash could do.

"Even The Skulls are vulnerable to internal bleeding and death." Sandy looked ill as she turned her back to what was happening.

"Lash," Angel said, grabbing his hand. "Stop him."

Hardy stepped forward. "The beating the boy is getting is what he deserves, but Tiny is acting like this because of Eva. He has a right, but it'll kill him if he kills Nash."

Biting his lip, Lash couldn't handle his brother being hit. Charging past the rest of the Skulls, Lash grabbed Tiny off his brother.

"Let him go, Tiny. You've done enough." Lash faced his leader and one of his closest friends prepared to do whatever it took to save his brother.

"He almost killed Eva." Tiny spat on Nash. "Your woman is pregnant, and he brought drugs into my compound. He's fucking finished."

"I can get him clean. This is not like Nash at all."

"Of course it is. He's the weakest one here. The fucker needs a wakeup call, and The Skulls are not for the weak."

Running a hand down his face, Lash looked at his brother. If Tiny kicked him out of the club, Nash would be as good as dead. All the shit his brother had caused would come crashing down on him. You were either a brother, or you were kicked to the curb.

There was only one way to keep him in the club.

"I'll take his beating for him. I'll vouch for him." Lash faced Tiny prepared to do everything that would guarantee his brother's safety. If he was going to get his ass kicked, then Nash was getting the detox, but Lash would be the one to handle it.

The brothers looked at him.

"Why's he getting the beating?" Killer asked.

"Lash is vouching to keep his brother in, which means the punishment needs to be paid. He needs to take the beating on Nash's behalf to keep him inside," Murphy said.

"No, he's done nothing wrong," Angel said.

Lash glanced toward his woman, seeing the tears in her eyes. Murphy held her back with Sandy trying to talk to her. "He's my brother, and I'm not leaving him alone in the dark. It'll kill him."

"You're prepared to take the beating for him?"

"Yes," Lash said, tightening his hands into fists. *You owe me fucking big time, brother.*

"Lash, no," Angel said. Her voice rose up to meet him. Looking at Tiny, he saw the resolve. This beating needed to come into order. There had been too much shit going down in the last year for anything to slide.

Raising his hand in the air, he asked for two minutes without actually speaking.

Tiny nodded, turning away.

Walking back to where his woman was being held by Murphy, he cupped her face, glaring at the other man to let her go.

"You can't do this, Lash. You do this, and he could kill you. I can't raise this baby alone."

"Can you get my brother into my car?" he asked, turning to Hardy. The other biker agreed and left.

"This is not right," Angel said. Tears were streaming down her face.

"It's right for this club—"

"Your stupid club shouldn't get to decide this."

Lash did the only thing he could to silence her. He slammed his lips down on hers. When she went lax in his arms, he pulled away.

"If Nash had raised that gun and aimed it at you, even accidentally like he did, I'd kill him. I wouldn't let him get away with hurting my woman. He's my brother, and I'd give him a beating of a lifetime." He looked over his shoulder to see Tiny waiting. "Eva belongs to Tiny. We all know it, and if anything happened to her, Nash wouldn't forgive himself. I'm doing this, and then I'm going to handle my brother." Caressing her cheek, he forced her to look at him. "But I'm going to need you to be strong for the both of us."

She sobbed, pressing her face against his chest. "I can do that."

"Good. Get her out of here, Murphy. She's not going to like this."

Angel fought Murphy. Lash walked away knowing Tate would console his woman. He went in front of Tiny and waited for the punishment to be dished out. The next couple of weeks were going to be fucking painful.

****

Sophia brushed some of her fringe away from her forehead as she stood packing more boxes. The job was so fucking boring, and she was tired again. All she wanted to do was curl back up around her pillow and go to sleep. Ever since her run in with Nash that was all she wanted to do, sleep. She'd not even been tempted to go to the club in case he was mean to her again.

Kate always had a mean thing to say about her.

Tears welled up in her eyes once again as memories of all the horrid things people had said to her over the years came crashing down. She really did wish she could cast the memories aside and start afresh.

Brushing away any evidence of tears, she continued working and contained her yawning. Willy came round, brushing up against her. She didn't give him the satisfaction of acknowledging his presence.

"What's the matter? Can't handle me, baby?" Willy asked.

Some of the workers laughed, and she looked around her. She turned to face him. "No, you couldn't handle me, and if you keep rubbing your little dick against my ass I'll sue you for sexual harassment." Sophia had enough of being pushed around, by him, by Kate, and even by Nash. She was done with it all.

The laughter died on his face. She turned away, going back to the boxes. The silence was deafening. Only the sound from the machines could be heard.

"Get back to work," Willy said, talking to the rest of the room.

She kept working even as he leaned in close. His foul breath brushed across her neck. "Sue me for sexual harassment all you want, Sophia. Just remember, I'll be the one who'll be walking away happy. No one is going to believe the sister of a whore."

Gritting her teeth, she kept assembling the boxes. *Money for rent. Money for rent.*

"You've not even got The Skulls on your side. I heard what happened at the diner. Your ass is not taken and not protected."

His hands caressed one cheek of her ass. "Think about that the next time you mouth off."

Before she could do anything he'd walked away. No amount of money was ever going to make her love this job. She hated this job and the people inside it. It fucking sucked. Blocking everything out, she focused on getting her shift done.

The work was mundane, which let her think about the one big problem in her life, Nash. She missed him so much. When she'd sent him away after he kissed her, she'd not thought through her actions at all. She'd simply reacted to what happened. The kiss had made her body react in ways she didn't know were possible. No other man had affected her the easy way that Nash did. Nothing had been easy to her, nothing. Her sister getting in with The Skulls had given them a layer of protection, or at least it had given Sophia some protection that she'd not seen at the time. Now, everything was gone, and she was considered free meat. Shaking her head, she pushed her fringe out of her eyes. She really needed to get her hair cut. It was too long, and the strands were becoming unruly.

Having any free time was not in the cards for her right now. Her life consisted of work and more work. Life was easier when Kate brought in money, but then when her sister got hooked on drugs, there was no money either.

Closing her eyes, she took several deep breaths before continuing with her job. At lunch she sat by herself ignoring all the looks she was getting. She'd never realized how much The Skulls had her back. Her sister shacking up with Nash made her life easier.

Sophia couldn't stop the stab of pain piercing her heart as she remembered the number of times she caught Nash and Kate together. Part of her always thought Kate did it on purpose. It was as if her sister knew that Sophia had a crush on Nash, and getting her to see them together was Kate's way of showing her that she didn't have a chance with him.

The logic was messed up, but it was the only thing she could think of to excuse Kate's actions.

She's gone.

Biting her lip she went back to work in a foggy haze. There were times she missed her older sister and other times when she was glad Kate was dead.

When it was time for her to finish work, she left the factory floor and grabbed her bag from her locker. Without looking at anyone she set off outside of the factory on her walk back home. Once she got home, she'd have a few minutes to wash, change and head out toward the diner.

Her life was not that eventful, but she got stuff done quickly. Hitching her bag high on her shoulder she kept her head down. The roads were rarely busy where the factory was located.

A couple of cars and trucks passed on their way into town.

Pulling the band out of her hair, she let the locks roam free. She wanted to feel the wind in her face before she was trapped in another building serving someone. There were no other jobs in Fort Wills, and she wasn't going to follow in her sister's footsteps. The sound of a car pulling up alongside her forced Sophia to stop.

Gill, along with a couple of his friends, was sat staring at her.

She started to walk away once again. The sound of doors opening travelled to her ears. Her heart sped up, and she focused on the path in front of her. The stretch where they'd stopped was the most deserted with no houses or buildings in sight. This was the part of the walk she hated. Anything could happen to her, and no one would know unless she was lucky enough for a car to pass.

Sophia knew she wasn't that lucky.

"Hey, why are you rushing?" Gill asked.

Walking faster she tried to avoid him. Gill grabbed her arm stalling her walking. He pushed her against the metal fence behind her.

"I've got a job to do. Leave me alone."

In the next breath he tore the bag from her shoulders throwing it at one of his friends. She recognized all of them but didn't know their names. It wasn't high on her list of activities to know the men who were working in the same building as she was.

Smart move, Sophia.

"I don't like your attitude. I mean, I was friends with your sister, and I'm sure I can extend the same kindness to you." He caressed down her cheek. His touch repulsed her.

When his hand made to touch her breast, she swatted it away. "Don't touch me."

She pushed him hard. Gill came back, slapping her around the face and shoving her harder against the metal barrier. Her back hurt from the slam, and she cried out. His friends were closing in around them, stopping anyone from seeing anything if someone was to pass.

"Now, I'm trying to be nice to you, and all you're doing is pushing me away." Gill wrapped his fingers around her throat, squeezing. She clawed at his hands trying to push him away.

Another hand landed between her thighs.

"I've been nice and patient with you, Sophia, but my patience is running out."

He tightened his hold between her legs making her wince. There was nothing gentle about him.

"Now, I'm going to let go. I want you to tell me what I want to hear." His hand released her throat.

She took deep gasps of breath, needing the air. Bending forward, she tried to clear her thoughts. Sophia wouldn't give him the satisfaction of making her beg.

"I'm waiting, Sophia," he said, running his hands down her back. He didn't have the right to touch her. No man had the right to touch her just because Kate wanted it. She didn't. Her body was her own, and she was nothing like her sister. It was time she started to remember that. She and Kate were two different people.

Standing up, holding her head high, she glared at him. "Fuck you."

The backhand took her by surprise, along with the thump to the stomach. She spit out some blood as she tasted the metallic flavor on her tongue. No one had ever hurt her like this.

Grabbing her hair, Gill spun her around, pushing her against the metal fence. Her breasts hurt from the bite.

Sophia panicked as he worked at her belt. "I'm going to fuck you so hard, and then my men are going to take you. Again, and again until you're begging us to stop—"

A shot rang out followed by a scream. She was released, and she turned in time to see Lash with three men hitting Gill and his friends.

"You touch Skull property, and I'll fucking kill you. Consider this your warning," Lash said, firing his weapon through the of one of the friends. Sophia winced while inside cheering at Lash's punishment. "Get the fuck out of here before I start snapping necks. I don't give a fuck who you are, but you better make sure I never find out." The threat was a real one. Everyone knew Lash had killed Angel's father by snapping his neck. Lash was one tough biker, and no one messed with him.

She got a good look at him and saw several bruises on his face. He was also using his left hand rather than his right. Lash looked in pretty bad shape.

"Get Nash to where I told you and keep him out of it," Lash said, giving out orders. The other two biker men left, leaving them alone.

Sophia stared at the gun in his hand, wondering if she was next on the list of people to go.

NASH

Chapter Four

Sophia stared at Nash's brother. The gun at his side terrified her. He'd shot someone in the leg and showed no remorse. Not to mention the many guys he'd killed in the protection of the club.

"Are you going to use that on me?" she asked, bending down to grab her bag. She had nothing to protect herself with. If he was going to use that, then she'd be completely helpless to whatever he had planned.

Lash looked at the gun then at her. "No, I'm not going to use it. I find it helps weaken a man intent on rape."

She flinched, recalling Gill's hands on her body. Lash hadn't needed to stop to protect her, but he had. "Thank you. I don't know what would have happened if you hadn't showed up."

"I know what would have happened. It doesn't take a rocket scientist to know what they all had on their minds."

"Thank you either way," she said, wiping the blood from her lip. Her body ached in ways she didn't like. She knew in a matter of minutes the places where Gill hit her would be badly bruised.

"Don't thank me. I may not be here for when it happens again."

His words made her pause.

"Again?"

"Yeah. A sick fuck like that, he wants you badly enough, he'll try again."

Sophia stared at her savior waiting for him to say something that would protect her. "I'm not strong enough, and I need that job," she said when he made no move to say or do anything else.

Lash kept staring at her without saying a word. She started to fidget, hating his scrutiny.

"My brother thinks you're an innocent one," Lash said.

"What?"

"Angel was purely innocent. I know. You're not. There's something about you that shows experience." He stepped forward grabbing her chin. "But you're not full of experience. Nash sees that side of you. He thinks you're weak enough that you can't handle the life of being an old lady."

She tugged out of his hold. "I'm not too innocent, and it's none of your goddamn business."

"Nash got his ass kicked today. He's hanging by a thread, and Tiny's this close to kicking his ass to the curb and out of the club life forever." He pressed his thumb and finger close together.

"Is he all right?"

"No, he's not all right. I made a deal to keep Nash in The Skulls. You want protection then you help me now," Lash said.

"I don't know what you want."

"I'm about to get Nash back on his feet. It's not going to pretty, but if you care about him, then you can help. In return you get The Skulls back for your protection, and no man will touch you." He stepped forward blocking her in.

"I'm not a sweet-butt or an old lady."

"I know. Sweet-butts earn their keep by giving us what we want. You're no sweet-butt. You'll help me with my brother, or you can see Gill and his goons in your future." Lash rested a hand against the metal, leaning in close. His closeness was unnerving her, and she knew he was doing it all on purpose. "If you don't help me then the next time I won't stop. I'll make sure everyone knows you're not under The Skulls' protection, and you're free meat."

"But Nash—"

He pressed a finger to her lips. "But Nash nothing. He won't have any say, and I don't give a fuck about you. You're not important to me, and I will make sure you get hurt."

The look in his eyes made her very aware of how he'd leave her behind.

"What do you want me to do?" she asked.

Sophia didn't need any further warning. She needed The Skulls a lot more than they needed her.

"Get on the back of my bike and come with me," Lash said. "No questions asked."

He didn't let her respond. She watched him walk to his bike and straddle the machine. "Are you getting on?"

She rushed toward his bike, straddling the machine.

"Wrap your arms around me, and I want you to make sure this is not a come on. I've got my wife, and she's plenty woman for me. I'm not cheating on her," he said.

She didn't expect anything else. Angel was a beautiful woman, and she saw why Lash loved her.

Wrapping her arms around his waist, Sophia closed her eyes and ignored the fact she wasn't wearing a helmet. No way would she ever get on the back of a bike unless there was a helmet present.

Sophia held him tightly, not wanting to let go of the security he gave her. They didn't speak. Words were not necessary as he worked the roads.

Only when the bike slowed down to a stop did she open her eyes. Before her was an old factory. It wasn't on multiple floors like the one she worked in. The "sold" sign on the outside of the building was glaring at her.

"Where are we?" she asked, climbing off the back of his bike and falling on her ass. Lash climbed off and helped her to her feet.

"It's the old factory ten miles from Fort Wills. A couple of years ago it was the food packing factory. The Skulls picked it up cheap, but we've not done anything with it." Lash headed toward the door.

"I know. The crash sent this place under. A lot of jobs were lost that day."

He agreed. "We're going to get it open. With all the guns pointed at our heads we've put off doing anything with it. Now, it's waiting for some use."

She followed behind him. He held a set of keys and typed in a number to the lock. The heavy door clicked and opened.

"It may be abandoned, but it's fucking secure."

Sophia had noted the large truck parked outside as well. Were they meeting someone? She was surprised to see the factory in working order. There were no musty smells or crumbling walls.

Lash helped her into the old fashioned elevator and clicked the button. She grabbed the side rails to hold on. Elevators and escalators terrified her. Anything that took her feet off the ground without her using them scared her. He smirked.

The elevator came to a stop, and Lash helped her off. She was embarrassed by the sweatiness of her palms. Rides like that always made her nervous. What if the elevator stopped?

Breathe, Sophia, breathe.

"You made it." Another biker with the same cut as Lash was stood at the far end of the floor. She saw another door just behind him.

"Did he cause you any trouble?" Lash asked.

"Not once. He's in a lot of pain. Sandy's checking him over now to make sure nothing is going to kill him." The man looked at her. "So why did we help the chick? She's no sweet-butt."

"Hardy, this is Sophia. You should remember her. She's Kate's sister."

The biker, known now as Hardy, stared hard at her. "She's nothing like her sister."

"You'll be the first person to think that," she said.

"Attitude's the same. You're looking pretty messed up. No guy should force a woman. Wish I killed that bastard now," Hardy said.

Lash remained silent, but something passed between the two bikers. "Let's get this done," Lash said.

He opened the door. Sophia saw it was dark. There was a large mattress against the wall. She spotted a bloodied and bruised Nash shivering on top of it.

"Nash," she said, starting to go to him.

"I don't think so, missy," another biker said.

"Zero, hold her. She can't go to him yet until I lay down the ground rules." Lash walked over to the opposite wall.

"What are you going to do?" Sandy asked. The blonde woman was stood with her arms folded. The other woman wasn't wearing much, just a short miniskirt and a tight shirt displaying most of her boobs.

"Nash is about to get the Lash detox treatment."

She saw him bend down into his box and retrieve a pair of metal cuffs.

"Shouldn't you put him in a rehab facility?" Sophia asked.

All the men laughed.

"Usually we'd go the rehab route, but my brother wouldn't last in there. He'd have the nurses eating his dick by the end of the day. Tiny won't put up the money either. Nash is going to get my cold, harsh treatment. I just took a beating to keep him in the club. He'll take my kind of treatment or die fucking doped." Lash moved toward his brother.

"Lash," Nash said.

"Shut the fuck up." Lash worked the chains around the bolts in the wall. Sophia could tell they were sturdy. Lash applied both cuffs to his brother's wrists, securing him in place. He walked away coming toward her. Sophia couldn't take her eyes off Nash. He looked so weak and frail.

"Do you really think this is necessary?" she asked, hating the sight of Nash strung up like that.

"A couple of hours ago he almost shot Eva through the head for having a little fun. He called my woman a slut, and I'm not settling with that." Lash looked back. "This is how I'm going to save my brother, not some half-cocked plan with a fucking therapist."

"Fine. You're the boss," she said.

"Good. I've called the diner and quit for you as well as the box factory. Your time if going to be spent here, taking care of him." Lash nodded to a guy behind her. "When we're done here, you're going to go back to her apartment and get some supplies. She's not going anywhere but where I tell her."

"Why don't you tell me what you've got planned?" Sophia asked.

"Fine. He's not moving out of those restraints. My brother is strong, and he'll hurt anyone to get what he wants. No booze, no pain killers, no drugs. Everything has officially stopped. I'm not giving him what he wants. He gets water and porridge. Nothing else."

"What if this kills him?"

"It won't. We've got a doctor who says it should work," Lash said, pointing to Sandy.

"I didn't say it wouldn't be difficult."

"I don't care what it takes. I'm getting my brother back." He looked at Zero. "Take her back to her apartment. Use the truck and get some stuff."

"Will do." She was pulled from the room. Sophia looked at Nash, knowing she'd do everything in her power to bring back to her the man she knew.
****

"This is fucking crazy," Nash said. He stared up at his brother seeing the determination on Lash's face.

"It's a plan, and you're going to have to take it otherwise it's the end of the road for you. I'm not going to let that happen."

"I shouldn't be here. You know it, and so do I." Nash lay on the mattress feeling every single one of his pains.

"How is he?" Lash asked.

Out of the corner of his eye he watched his brother talking with the doctor. "He's in pretty bad shape. Tiny did a number on him. I don't think there's any internal bleeding. He may have a cracked rib, and I'll bring some bandages to help."

"Nothing for the pain. He's going to take this like he deserves."

"Don't you think that's a little extreme?" Sandy asked.

"If the gun had been aimed at your head, what do you think?"

Sandy didn't argue. "Fine. I'm going to go and give the others an update. If you need anything, give me a call. I'm here for you all."

She left through the door. The same door that Sophia had left through a couple of minutes before. He'd seen the cuts and bruises on her face. Who had hurt his woman?

"If you want to leave, you can," Lash said. The other two bikers gave him a sour look before turning away.

"You should have left me to rot," Nash said. "The club hates me." He rolled to his back, wincing in pain.

"I'm not giving up on you. The club is our whole lives. I'm not going to let you throw all that away because you think life is a little hard."

"A little hard? Brother, life is a damn hard fucking road and filled with pain."

Lash knelt beside the mattress. Guilt swamped Nash as he got a good look at the marks on Lash's face.

"You shouldn't have taken that beating for me."

"Did you expect me to let Tiny kill you?" Lash asked. "You're an ass, but you're still my baby brother."

He watched as his brother sat on the mattress beside him. A long time had passed since he'd been sat on a makeshift bed talking with his brother.

"I'm not worth saving. I'm the weak link."

His brother started laughing. "You think you're weak. It took 'til you were thirty to reach for the drugs. The booze and the women were who you were. I saw the way you treated Sophia for the brief moments you were with her." Lash reached out, taking his hand. "Someone who can love like that, is not weak."

Nash gritted his teeth as tears welled in his eyes. "You're turning me into a fucking pussy." He let the tears fall, feeling the misery of what his life had become. "It doesn't matter how much I love her. I hurt her the other day with the way I treated her."

"If Sophia cares about you, or even loves you a little bit, then she'll forgive you," Lash said.

"I don't know. I called her a whore. She's not a whore. She's special. Anyone with eyes should be able to see it." He gripped his brother's hand hard. It would only be a matter of time before the effect of the drugs ran off completely.

"You see it with Sophia like I see it with Angel."

"Why was she so bloody?" Nash asked, looking at his brother.

Lash looked down at the floor. "You're not going to want to hear this."

"I need to hear this. If you're going to do to me what I think you are, then I need something to keep me going, otherwise I won't survive this on my own." Nash coughed, wishing he'd dumped the first bag of white powder instead of finding solace in the stuff. His biggest fucking mistake was taking that shit. "I can take it, Lash."

"Your bank account has nothing in it, and the apartment you'd been paying for stopped. She had to find a second job. I got Whizz to look through your records. You're broke. The money you've been taking is club money, Nash. I've given Tiny back everything you took. It looks like along with the drugs you'd been gambling as well."

"Fuck. I made a big bet in a drug haze. I lost everything," Nash said, remembering. He'd been so out of it he'd not even thought about the money he was using to replace his losses. "I'll pay you back."

"Get sober first and drug free."

"What else? Tell me everything." Nash felt sick to his stomach. His brother was trying to keep something from him, and he was getting a bad feeling about it.

"Sophia quit college and works at the box factory and the diner."

"She's working two jobs?"

"Yeah, that's what she has been doing the past couple of months. I don't know what has been going on at work, but this afternoon she was attacked. I stopped them from really hurting her."

Nash sat up blocking the exploding pain inside his head. "Someone put their hands on my woman." The sight of her bruised face would haunt him forever.

"She's not been protected by The Skulls. Kate's dead, and Sophia's open to it now. This is why we protect our own. We're not leaving her alone again. She's agreed to help with you."

"Until I'm well you've got to promise me that you'll protect her. You'll do everything you can to keep her safe," Nash said, needing his brother's word that he would.

"Why do you think she's helping me with you? I'm keeping you both safe. I'm not losing either of you, and if I've got to do this all by myself then that's what I'm going to do." Lash stood up, moving away. "I'm going to make sure everything is working, and hopefully by then she'll be back."

His brother left the room, leaving the door open. Nash tested the restraints and was satisfied when they didn't budge.

"This fucking sucks."

Closing his eyes, Nash tried to think of something better than being chained to the wall in the factory. His thoughts always returned to Sophia.

He smiled as he recalled the first time he met her two years ago.

****

"I'm bored, Kate. Come on, let's head back to the club," Nash said. She'd sucked him twice, and he was ready to pound her pussy. Out of all of the sweet butts at The Skulls, Kate was the one who'd caught his eye.

"I just need to stop off home, and then we can head back to the club." She pulled out her keys, her hands shaking as she did.

He'd noticed Kate was not always with it. Nash put it down to all the alcohol the bitch consumed.

"Nice place you got here," he said. He wasn't drunk at all, but he found Kate stopped hassling him all the time if she thought he was. Nash thought it was funny to play the drunk rather than to be the actual drunk.

She flicked the light on and told him to shush. "My sister is home. Fat bitch never goes out. I bet she's eating ice cream and watching a movie wishing it was her."

Nash chuckled, not really seeing the humor. He'd not met Kate's sister. In his mind he pictured a fat version of Kate.

Sitting down on the sofa, he watched Kate bend down, looking for something. "Are you all right here? I've got to go and check some things out?" she asked.

"Yeah, I'm good here."

When she was out of sight, he put down the bottle of scotch Kate had carried and eased back against the sofa. The springs dug into his back. He doubted Kate earned enough to keep this place in good working order. If it wasn't for her talented mouth and hot pussy he wouldn't be interested in her.

"Kate? Is that you? I thought you said you were staying out tonight?" A feminine voice invaded his thoughts. Nash was shocked by the instant heat that flooded his groin. No woman had left him feeling like that. Getting up from his sofa he turned to see who it was.

The woman looked at him and frowned.

"I take it you're Sophia, Kate's sister," he said. She looked nothing like Kate. Her hair was tied on top of her head. The dark, midnight black curls contrasted with

her pale skin. Her flesh was flawless, not a mark on her. She had a cute nose and the sweetest eyes he'd ever seen.

She didn't wear an ounce of makeup, and she was currently wearing a pair of pajamas with chocolate chip cookies on them. The night clothes couldn't hide her fuller curves either. Her tits were large, and he wanted to see if she had red nipples or brown. Did she wax, or was she neatly trimmed?

All the wicked thoughts were going to his cock, making him want her.

"I'm sorry, I don't know who you are," she said, shaking his hand and pulling back. Sophia didn't linger on him or make any innuendos. He watched as she walked to the kitchen and filled the kettle.

"I'm Nash. I'm part of The Skulls."

"Is Nash your real name?" she asked, turning toward him. He couldn't hear Kate, and he didn't care. All need to be inside Kate disappeared. Moving toward the kitchen counter he took a seat.

"No, it's Edward. Edward Myers."

"It's lovely to meet you. Kate's told me a lot about you."

"I hope it's all good stuff." Nash folded his arms, wanting to impress her somehow.

Her eyes didn't move down his body. She stayed focused with looking at him.

"Yeah, she's very happy to have met you and been with you." Her cheeks turned a dark red, and she finished making a drink. "Do you want a drink?"

"I'd love one." Not one woman had ever offered him a drink before. It was strange, but Kate offered to fuck and suck his dick before she handed him a drink.

This was the newest experience to him, and it was odd.

The blush coating her cheeks drew him in as well. What was she embarrassed about?

"I see you've seen my chunky sister," Kate said, sitting beside him. Her hand wandered up the inside of his leg. He swatted her hand away and shot her a glare.

Anger at her calling Sophia names shot through him. With Sophia's back to him, he wrapped his fingers around Kate's throat. "Don't ever call her that again." He leaned in close pretending to kiss her. "Or I'll fucking end you and make sure no one can identify the body."

Pulling out of the memory, Nash coughed, wishing someone would just shoot him. The pain was too intense for him to handle, and he was finding it harder and harder to fight.

****

"You fucking promised me these boys would keep in line," Snitch said, slamming his fist on the table. He was camped in the warehouse waiting for the perfect opportunity to do what he'd come back to Fort Wills to do, and now his men were telling him the group of criminals they'd hired might have fucked it up. He was pissed, beyond pissed. He was fucking furious. "What exactly did Lash do?" It was taking every ounce of strength not to hurt one of his men.

"He caught the men trying to rape Sophia. They were in broad daylight—"

Snitch lost his temper, grabbing Scars around the neck and slamming him against the nearest wall. "I didn't give fucking permission for them to tease a woman, especially a woman so close to the fucking Skulls. We're waiting for the right time. Lash starts looking at those bastards, Tiny will know about me. We're doing this low key."

"It's just a bitch."

Snitch slammed his fist into Scars's stomach. "Nash is the weakest link. He's being taken out of the problem with the club. They've got him alone with his woman. He's vulnerable, and if he so much as starts thinking about shit, then we're done. You better pray that doesn't happen. Tiny never forgot about me. He acts like he does, but we've got a lot of history he wouldn't want his boys to know." Releasing his man, Snitch took a step back. "Call your men. You warn them that if they act without orders again, I will cut their balls off and feed their dicks to them."

Walking away, Snitch went outside breathing in the fresh air. Everything was so close. He wasn't going to let some common fucking thugs ruin everything he'd fought so hard to get.

The time for his revenge was close. Tiny was going down. Waiting was not the problem when he saw an end in sight.

Chapter Five

Sophia tapped her fingers on her thigh wishing for the day to be over. Her back was hurting from being slammed against the metal railings by Gill. Part of her wished she could go back and gouge the bastard's eyes out. Her nails sank into the denim of her jeans. She wanted to feel the pain to stop thinking about what the bastard could have done with her.

"You've surprised me," Zero said.

Turning toward him, she waited for him to elaborate. She'd never been alone with this Skull. Lash and Nash were the only Skulls she'd been alone with. He didn't make any move to say anything else.

"What do you mean?" she asked, needing to be distracted.

"I was there when those men had you trapped against the metal fence. A lot of women would have broken down by now. Not you. You're going strong." Zero nodded his head. "I respect that."

"I don't have time to panic about it. Nash needs my help, and Lash has agreed to protect me providing I help him." She'd do anything for Nash. Kate knew the truth of her feelings and spent a great deal of time taunting her about it.

"It's more than that. You're in love with Nash."

She didn't say anything to him. Speaking of her feelings would never be good for her. Kate made her life a misery because of her feelings. She remembered the time Kate brought him home and fucked him in the next room. Every time she saw Nash after that she'd been unable to look him in the eye.

"You don't have to say anything to me. I get it."

"I do love him. He's been good to me, and he was good for my sister." She turned to Zero. "I'm really sorry that Kate brought drugs into his life."

"It's not your fault. Nash should have stopped. He knows the rules, and this is entirely on him. You're not to blame no matter what you think." Zero reached over, squeezing her hand.

"Are you all this nice?"

Zero laughed. "Not many people would say we're nice."

She smiled. "You're being nice to me, and that's all I care about."

He pulled up outside of the apartment block, and she climbed out. Zero followed close behind her. She blanked the people who were watching her. It wasn't anyone's business with Zero being near her. She ran up the stairs with him close behind her.

Grabbing her set of keys out of the bag, she tried to put the key into the lock. Her hands were shaking so bad that she couldn't get it to fit. Cursing, she tensed as Zero took the keys from her.

"Thank you."

"I'm not going to hurt you. Stop thinking I am."

She pushed her way into her apartment and went straight to her bedroom. Sophia grabbed the case from inside her wardrobe and began to fill it with her clothes.

Zero stood in the doorway.

"Nash helped you to move, didn't he?"

"Yeah, he did."

"What happened between you two?" Zero asked.

"I don't want to talk about it."

"So you agree that something went down between the two of you."

She paused in putting clothes away and glanced at the tall man. Zero was a large man with plenty of muscles. His hair was cut tight to his head. She saw a tattoo coming out of his shirt and circling his neck.

"Nothing really happened. He was with Kate, and I told him I couldn't be with him."

"Is that bullshit I smell?"

Sophia didn't respond and started to put some clothes into a case. "He kissed me, and I freaked out. It was good, and I couldn't handle the thought of him being with my sister. I'd heard them plenty of times. It's wrong. I shouldn't have feelings for the guy my sister was with."

Shaking her head, she walked into the bathroom.

Zero followed her into the bathroom. "What are you doing?" she asked. He closed the door behind him.

His hand went to her hip, and he spun her to face him. "I was never with your sister. She was too fucking easy, and I thought I'd catch something."

"Do you think your feelings have something to do with Kate?" he asked.

"I don't understand what you're trying to say." Sophia nibbled her lip. Zero was too close to her.

Zero pressed her up against the counter. "What do you think I'm trying to do?" He invaded her space. His hand rested on her hip, pulling her in close. She felt the hard ridge of his cock pressing against her stomach.

Her heart was racing, and she didn't know why. There was no answering pulse in her groin, and she didn't feel turned on. If anything, she felt like this was going to be a big mistake.

"Don't overthink everything."

"This is not right."

He caught her lips underneath his. Nash's kiss, what she remembered of it, had been sweet and gentle. Nash had taken his time, opening her lips to receive him. Zero plundered away. There was no effort to his technique. He simply took what he wanted without waiting for her.

In no time at all his hands were wandering over her body, and she hated it.

Pulling away, she shook her head. "No, stop. I don't want this. This is not what I want from you." She pushed at his shoulders. Zero stepped back immediately. He didn't look offended or upset.

"If you want some advice, honey, stop pushing the boy away. Otherwise at the end of all of this, he's going to find a woman who really wants him and doesn't keep pretending she doesn't."

Sophia waited for him to leave before she got her shampoo and conditioner. She chanced a look in the mirror and winced when she saw the marks on her face. Kate never came home looking like this.

Pressing her hand to the glass she walked away, finishing her case. Zero had packed her fridge up and was eating a slice of the chocolate cake she'd baked the night before.

"Did you make this, or is this one of the shop bought crappy ones?" Zero asked.

"I baked it."

"You're a damn fine cook."

"You've not tried my food yet. A cake is not a good thing to judge on."

"If you cook like this then you're all right by me. I might even put a good word in for you with Tiny."

She snorted. "I doubt he'll want anything to do with me. He'll probably hold me responsible for one of his men going off the rails."

Zero finished his slice of cake, taking the whole thing with him. "You'll be surprised. Tiny wouldn't hold you responsible at all." He walked toward the door. "Any man who becomes a Skull has to take on the job of being strong enough to handle what anyone throws at them. Nash needs to be strong no matter what bitch stands in his way. What's the point of having men who can't fight when their pussy's being difficult?"

"Do you have to speak like that?" she asked.

"Get used to it, baby. We're not here to make everything a fairy tale. We work hard and party hard. We fuck who we want and don't give a fuck about what people think. You want Nash then you're going to have to start playing by their rules."

She was close behind him as he made his way out of the building. Sophia noticed him holding the butt of his gun on the way to the truck. "Do you expect us to be attacked?"

"If word spreads about Nash enemies could think we're weak. I'm not about to be jumped for the kid making a mistake. He has serious issues, but what Lash is about to put him through is going to be hell." Zero pushed her up in the truck.

Putting on the seat belt she waited for Zero to get in the driver's seat.

"What do you mean hell?"

"You don't think Lash is going to let his brother get away with him taking a beating? Lash is going to make sure Nash pays. Tiny and the whole of the club are going to need proof that Nash is making recompense and that his recovery is as painful as possible."

Her eyes were wide as she stared at him. They had to be wide. She'd never heard anything so barbaric in her whole life.

"They're brothers. Why can't you accept that?"

Zero steered the truck to the side of the road. "Listen, sweet cheeks, we're the ones responsible for this town. We make sure you can walk down the street safely, or in your case as safely as you can. We keep the shit out of the town. If Tiny starts taking anyone on, our enemies would be on us like flies 'round shit. Deal with it. This is how we handle club business. You can't handle it then I suggest you get the fuck out of the way."

She licked her lips. Her throat had gone dry. "I'm not going to like what Lash is going to do to his brother, am I?" she asked.

"No, you're not. If you know what's good for you, you'll turn away and do exactly what Lash demands."

Zero pulled the truck back onto the main road.

She didn't speak for the rest of the journey. When they parked up outside of the factory, Lash was smoking a cigarette and talking on the phone.

"I'm okay, baby. I've got everything covered. I'll be there tonight, and we'll talk about it. Nash is fine, and I'll take care of him."

Sophia grabbed her case and started walking toward him. She was conscious of Zero following behind her.

"I love you, too. Bye." Lash hung up, facing her. He looked at the case. "Is that it?"

"I don't have a lot of stuff." She shrugged.

"I brought her food. Bitch is one good baker." Zero was guarding the chocolate cake as if it was an expensive jewel.

"Good, let's get set up."

Lash headed into the factory.

****

Opening his eyes, Nash saw his brother leading Sophia back into the room. One of her hands was holding her side, and she was carrying a case with her.

"She going to be my babysitter?" Nash asked.

"Yep, I thought I was being kind."

"Then you're fucking wrong. You want to get me sober and off the drugs get her away from here." He saw her flinch, and he hated causing her any kind of pain. "She's too weak to handle what you're going to throw at me."

Lash looked at Sophia then back at him. "You really think so?"

"She's innocent, Lash. Don't put her through this."

Zero snorted, and Lash chuckled.

He watched as his brother advanced on him. "I think it's time you open your eyes up about your woman, brother." Lash grabbed a fistful of Nash's hair. "Take a good long look at her. She's no innocent. I'm not calling her a whore. Sophia's strong, Nash. She's no weakling, and if anyone's going to help you, it's her."

She cleared her throat. "Where do I put my stuff?"

"Through to the other room. Zero will get you settled. I've made everything so you'll be comfortable for your stay."

Sophia stared at Nash. He couldn't tear his gaze away from her. Standing to his feet, he glared at her, hating the fact she was seeing him like this. The cuffs his brother had bound his wrists with had enough give for him to move to the edge of the mattress. The cuffs must have come from some kind of BDSM shop, especially designed to bind a person yet allow *some* movement. The chains were locked into hooks in the wall. Nash gave his brother credit for style. He never thought he'd see the day when he was bound to the fucking wall with kinky cuffs. Fortunately, he wasn't completely bound with his back against the wall.

"Do you see anything you like?" he asked, opening his arms wide.

Stop it, Nash. This is not what you want.

He couldn't stop it.

Her eyes narrowed. "No, I don't." She took a step close then closer still. The heels of her boots clicked on the floor with her advancing steps. He was at the edge of the mattress. The chains on his wrists gave him a little moving room. Not much, but enough to not make him feel trapped. She'd never looked at him with anything other than happiness.

Sophia glanced up and down at his body. "You don't think I can handle what you've got to throw at me."

"You're not prepared for The Skulls' approach to life, baby. You can't handle anything."

His lack of faith in her being able to handle the life was why he'd never tried anything else on her.

"You think I'm too innocent even though I heard you fucking my sister?" Sophia asked.

Nash didn't break eye contact even though he wanted to. He kept looking at her waiting for her to cower away from him.

She chuckled. "You really think I'm sweet and innocent."

There was something about her voice that made Nash stay quiet.

"Then what do you think now?"

He watched her walk toward Zero. Sophia dropped her bag to the floor along with her jacket. The sway of her hips captured his gaze. The bangles on her wrists gave an edge to her appearance. He wanted his hands on her hips and wanted to feel that lush body against his own.

She ran her hands up Zero's chest.

Jealousy gripped every part of him, and he tensed in the restraints. Sophia turned so he got a good view and plundered her tongue into Zero's mouth. His biker brother ran his hands over her body, squeezing that full ass.

He jerked to try to get to her. Nash was held in place.

When she withdrew her lips were swollen. She turned to him and started toward him. Sophia grabbed her backpack and then invaded his personal space. "The only person who can't deal with me being part of The Skulls, is you. You could have me a long time ago, but you wanted my sister. I wasn't ready to get over you with my sister. I didn't want that, but I still wanted you to be my friend. I'm not the person you think I am, Nash. It's time you opened your eyes."

"I'm not a fucking mind reader," Nash said, yelling the words.

"Well, now you know the truth. I'm here, and I'm waiting for you to get over yourself."

She didn't wait for him to respond before she was on her way.

"You've just had your ass handed to you, *Edward*," Zero said.

"Touch her again and I'll cut your balls off. She's mine."

Zero smirked. "You're in no position to question me. I'll go and see if she's getting settled."

He had to watch Zero walk toward Sophia. Yanking at the chains, Nash let out a growl. He couldn't handle watching one of his brothers taking on Sophia.

Fuck, the look in her eyes would stay with him forever. In all the time he'd known her, he'd never once seen her look sexy. She'd always been beautiful to him but too innocent to ever explore.

Had she ever really been innocent?

Crap, his thoughts were all over the place, and he couldn't think clearly at all.

"What are you thinking?" Lash asked.

His brother was stood with his arms folded over his chest.

"These restraints are fucking unnecessary." He pulled on them hoping they'd pull away easily. Nothing happened. Until Lash opened them up this was where he was staying.

"Do you really think I'm going to believe that?" Lash stared at him, smirking.

"You're being an asshole. It's my least favorite quality about you." Nash stopped pressing on the restraints and sat down on the makeshift bed. "Is this what you're going to do to save me?" He laughed. "This is the worst fucking idea in the world." Nash wiped his brow free of sweat.

"We'll see who is laughing in a couple of weeks. When did you start using?" Lash sat down opposite him.

The desire to lie filled every part of him. "Why do you want to know?"

"I want to know when my brother started going off the rails. I need to know what I'm fighting against."

Letting out a breath, he rested his arms on his knees. "Fine. The day I moved Sophia into her apartment we kissed, and she told me she couldn't. She kicked me out with a box of Kate's possessions. I found a little white bag of powder and figured I'd give oblivion ago."

"Then you fucked over your life. Beating up drug dealers and making sure everyone knew The Skulls had a patched in member who couldn't keep his shit together. Thanks a lot." Lash stood up, going toward the fridge in the room.

"You're welcome."

The beer Lash was holding was thrown across the room where it smashed on the opposite wall, the ale spilling down the wall as the glass lay broken to pieces.

"It's not fucking funny, *Edward*. Alex is already having to deal with the fucking backlash from your incompetence."

Nash didn't say a word. He kept his gaze on Lash's without looking away.

"You don't give a shit about the club, fine." His brother stopped glancing toward the open door where Sophia had disappeared. "Every day you spend here fighting me and what I'm about to do, she's going to be here. Sophia is going to be here with Zero, Butch, even Whizz and Time. All of the brothers are going to be here on babysitting duty."

"What's your fucking point?" Gritting his teeth, Nash spat the words out.

"She's a hot piece of ass. I'm sure many of our men would *love* a piece of her." Lash licked his lips, giving the door a pointed look.

"You've got Angel."

"And Murphy has Tate. The other men, they've got a sweet-butt. I think one of them if not all would love a chance to take Sophia out for a little spin. She'll be a fucking wild woman." Lash got up. "Think about that."

Nash felt sick to his stomach. There was no way he could survive if one of his brothers started to worm their way into Sophia's life. She was his woman. The reason he'd not already put a gun to his temple. Sophia was a fuller woman, rounded in all the right places. The guys would love her. He knew it in his heart and soul. It hadn't taken him long to fall in love with her from that first meeting.

They wouldn't do that to me.

Biting his lip, he stared at the door waiting for them to come back. He couldn't hear a thing, and his body was starting to shake. Shit, how long had it been since he'd had a hit?

81

Don't think about it.

Rolling up in a ball, he stared at the door, hoping and wishing they'd all come out and put him out of his misery.

Nothing happened, not one thing.

****

Lash walked into the other room to see Sophia putting away some of her clothes and Zero watching her. The hunger on the biker's face surprised him. He'd only been testing his brother, but seeing the lust plainly on Zero's face started a plan rolling. Sophia was completely oblivious to the attention she was getting.

"How is he?" Sophia asked, putting the last item of clothing in the wardrobe he'd purchased.

He'd always intended to intervene in his brother's mess. Angel had picked out the furniture for the room.

"Cursing, ranting, being a bastard because he knows what annoys me." Lash picked up the stuffed teddy from the floor.

She grabbed it out of his hands and placed the teddy on the bed. He wasn't going to say a word at all. Angel still owned a teddy from her childhood days. The stuffed gorilla sat on a shelf along with some books in their bedroom. Women were freaky creatures.

"He's your brother. Nash is going to know everything about you."

"Yeah, I've got an idea though. When you go out there I don't want you to call him Nash."

Zero stood up.

"Why not?" Sophia asked.

"Nash is his biker name. By his actions, he's not a Skull. It's time for him to know the true extent of what he's done."

"So he's Edward or fucker," Zero said.

"That's pretty colorful." Sophia smiled anyway.

"We'll give him everything he's earned." Lash stared at Sophia knowing jealousy could help them bring his brother back. This woman had given his brother a reason to be better. He'd seen the love in Edward's eyes when she came into their world all those months ago. If it was up to his brother, the men who put the marks on her face would be dead.

"You've got a plan?" Zero asked.

"Yeah. He's not going to like it, but I think it could help."

"Why do I feel I'm not going to like it?" Sophia asked.

"Because you're not. I'm going to need you to be strong through this." Lash waited for her confirmation.

"I will. I can do this. Nash, I mean, Edward, has always been there for me when he didn't have to be. I owe him this."

"He's jealous around you, Sophia. When you kissed Zero, he was angry. He wanted to hurt him. I need you to make him jealous and to make him want to fight."

Sophia started laughing. "You really think making Edward jealous is the key to waking him up. To keeping him alive and free from drugs?"

"By having the other Skulls here he'll see them with you. I'll let them all know it's just an act. You don't have to fuck any of them to get me what I want. You'll make sure Edward is nothing on the drugs." Lash caught her face in his hands. "Do you want my brother and I don't mean as a friend?"

"Yes." The word was a mere whisper, but he caught it.

"Then you need to make him believe he's got a shot with you. All Edward has ever wanted is you. Kate was a means to be with you."

"You're reaching," Sophia said.

"I'm not. Give him the idea you two could be together. Don't bring your insecurities into this. Be the woman you want to be, and then Edward will fight this."

They were all silent for a moment.

"Okay, fine, I'll do this, but you better make sure all of your men know I'm not fair game."

Sophia pushed past him heading toward the other room.

"You're being serious about this?" Zero asked.

"What's the matter? Afraid you can't handle it?"

"I can handle anything the club throws at me. I just hope Sophia can handle Edward. This is going to be a tough couple of weeks."

Lash nodded. "You can flirt, kiss, even stroke her, but don't go too far. Sophia is taken."

Zero held his hands up. "I wouldn't cause any harm."

"I saw the way you were looking at her. Don't."

While Edward was still in the club, even barely, Lash was going to look out for his brother and protect what was his, even his woman.

Chapter Six

Sophia watched as Edward shook on the mattress. Lash had left a couple of hours ago, and Zero was sat beside her. The biker had taken the first night watch with her. She'd never seen Edward like this. Leaning forward onto her knees she fought the urge to go to him. Lash had forbidden any comfort. It was horrid, and she hated not comforting him.

"Are you all right?" Zero asked.

While she watched the man on the mattress, she felt his eyes on her.

"I'm fine. I've got to be fine. This is all I've got left to do. Lash has seen to that."

"Do you really think you can walk away after this?"

"I don't know." She turned to look at him. "I've got to take Lash's opinion that we can fix Edward and that he wants me. Last time I checked the world doesn't work that way."

Running fingers through her hair she stood up heading toward the stove. She poured some milk into a pan.

"I'll have a hot chocolate," Zero said.

She went about making them both a hot chocolate.

"I saw Nash, not Edward, with Kate. He couldn't stand her half the time, but whenever that woman mentioned she needed to go home and if someone would give her a ride, he was always there. No one was allowed to take her home but him."

Stirring the chocolate into the milk she stared straight ahead of her. "What are you trying to say?"

"He was getting there to be with you. When you came to the club that day badly bruised, he was beside himself. You're everything to him, Sophia." She turned and handed him the cup of hot chocolate. "You may not think it, but I know you can get him through this."

"What if this radical detox doesn't work? We don't even know why he got addicted in the first place."

"We're getting the drugs out of his system, and then we're going to see about everything else. Lash won't go easy on his brother."

She sat down, taking a sip of the chocolate. An empty bowl lay beside the mattress ready for when he vomited. She'd placed a blanket around him to make sure he wasn't too cold.

"I wish this had never happened."

"It did, and now we're dealing with the consequences of that. Lash knows his brother better than anyone."

She nodded, watching the bed again. This was the first time she'd spent a great deal of time with any of his friends.

"What was Kate like at the club?" she asked, turning to him.

Zero looked uncomfortable. "You don't want to know."

"He spent a lot of time with her away from me. I need to know what he saw in her, if he saw anything at all."

"She fucked everyone, Sophia. Her mission in life was to have all of The Skulls' dicks inside her. I wasn't into her, and she hated me for it. Edward just gave it to her because she was easy."

Tears welled in her eyes. "Thank you."

"What? Why?"

"I needed to hear that. You've just confirmed I'm nothing like my sister. I couldn't sleep around, and I don't make it my life's ambition to fuck everyone. Thank you."

"You're one strange chick."

She finished her drink. "I'm going to get some sleep. I'll see you in the morning."

"I've got a bed in there as well. I'll give you twenty minutes for privacy."

"Okay." She left him alone, going through to the other room. In the corner, far enough away from the bed was where one of the Skulls was going to sleep when they stayed with her at night. She missed her apartment, the comfort of being off the floor.

Pulling her clothes off she quickly put on her nightclothes and climbed under the sheets. Without fail Zero walked in twenty minutes later. She watched him put his gun on the floor beside him and start to strip. Turning away, she gave him the privacy he deserved and closed her eyes.

In the other room she heard Edward whimper. Biting her lip, she stayed in bed waiting for sleep to claim her. This was the first time she'd been about to sleep in a room with a man.

She wasn't completely innocent like Edward thought she was. She'd had sex before but had never actually spent all night in bed with a man. After the appalling sex she'd left the guy's room immediately, not wanting to see him again. The first time was supposed to be the worst.

The sex had been so bad she'd not even gone looking for more.

Soon she felt sleep claim her.

The sound of vomiting and screaming woke her up. Jerking up in bed, it felt like she'd just fallen asleep. She scurried out of bed. Zero was also getting out of bed.

Going through to the other room, she found Edward puking into the bowl she'd left. She didn't wait for Zero to tell her what to do. Charging for the bed, she wrapped her arms around his back, stroking his hair.

"Let it all out. I've got you, Edward."

He grumbled but didn't say anything.

"You shouldn't be holding him, Sophia," Zero said.

She looked up glaring at him. "Lash didn't say anything about not being there for him. I'm holding him, which is what everyone deserves when they're ill."

Edward wasn't all that conscious either. She could tell from the way he was acting. His body was covered with sweat, and the scent of the vomit was making her sick to her stomach. When he was finished, she left his side instantly even though he reached toward her.

"I need something. It hurts."

"You're not getting anything, pal," Zero said.

"I wasn't fucking talking to you."

"Come on, Sophia, please." He was looking at her with doggy eyes. Sad doggy eyes at that. She cleared away the bowl, wiped away the spillage, and grabbed his chin harshly.

"You're not getting anything from me but a fucking bowl of porridge. You've been a bad little bear." She shoved him away and walked off even as he started to curse her, calling her names.

Blocking everything out, she went back to bed, holding onto her teddy as if it was a lifeline. Minutes later Zero walked into the room. Within moments he was settling behind her.

She tensed. "What the hell are you doing?" she asked.

"I'm not going to try anything with you. It seems you need a hug. I'm offering you comfort, Sophia, without any crap."

She turned toward him seeing the sincerity on his face. Slowly his arms wrapped around her. Sophia didn't want to fight him and curled in close.

Not been alone with a man and now you're sleeping next to one you don't know. Classy.

"He doesn't mean anything he's saying. It's the drugs. The detox makes you do crazy shit."

"I did this, Zero. I pushed him away, and it has been a big regret. I love him, and I shouldn't have done what I did."

"He should have been stronger. Yeah, you pushed him away, but you didn't force the fucking drugs up his nose. Do you really think you could have stopped him with that?" Zero asked.

"I don't know." She closed her eyes, enjoying being held even if it was by someone she barely knew.

"Thank you for being here with me," she said.

"There's nowhere else I'd rather be."

When she next woke up it was to see Lash staring down at them. "I see you two had a busy night."

Sophia blinked the sunlight out of her eyes becoming aware of Zero lying right close behind her, along with the evidence of his happiness to be that close. Jumping out of bed she headed toward the kitchen without looking back. There was nothing going on between her and Zero. She didn't even know why the other biker was being so nice to her. Zero's kindness and attention were unnerving her.

Edward was sat on the bed. He was pale and looked like shit. When he stared up there were tears in his eyes. Shooting him a glare, she started to work on the breakfast. Another biker was sat at the table, and she jumped back.

"Who are you?" she asked.

"I'm Killer." The man was larger than Lash and looked far more deadly. "I'm taking over for Zero." There was no way she was letting this giant cuddle up against her. Fuck, she shouldn't have let Zero cuddle against her. There was no way she wanted him getting the wrong idea about her.

"Did you sleep well?" Edward asked.

She nodded, not meeting his eyes.

"Well I had a great night's sleep," Zero said, walking through. His hand lingered on her hip as he kissed her cheek. "It's just for show." He whispered so only she could hear.

Chancing a look at Edward she saw he was tense and his hands were tight fists.

Putting together some food for the bikers she finished Edward's porridge last. "Here you go, Edward," she said, handing him the bowl.

"What happened to Nash?"

It was the first time he'd asked about the name change. She felt the men behind her were ready to take over. Bending down to his level, she stared him in the eye. "Nash is part of The Skulls. He's not a druggie or an addict. You're not him."

Turning away from him she walked into the bedroom to get changed. None of the men came through, which she was thankful for. When she was done, she ate her own porridge before finishing the dishes she'd used.

"I'm staying today," Lash said. "You can go until tonight." He spoke to the other men waiting for their instructions.

Zero and Killer left the building leaving her alone with the two brothers. From the look Lash was giving his brother, it was going to be a long day.

Going through to the other room she grabbed a book and went to sit down at the table. Every now and again she winced as Lash landed a blow to his brother. When he released the cuffs binding him to the wall she was surprised.

They fought, hard. Edward didn't get many blows in. It took everything inside her not to stop what was happening. She needed to trust Lash that he knew what he was doing.

Sophia hoped she could stick it out to make Edward better. She hated seeing him ill.
****

That night Edward was chained to the wall. He'd already thrown up everything he'd eaten, but the shaking was the worst. Edward hated the shaking more than anything else. Every now and then he looked at the door separating him from Sophia. Killer had left him an hour ago, and he couldn't help but wonder what the hell was going on beyond that door.

Don't think about it.

Zero had made sure he knew about his interest. Sophia was his woman.

You don't deserve her.

He needed her though. With Sophia close he felt like his whole world was complete. The only problem he found was the fact he couldn't reach out and touch her. She was there, but when he spoke to her, shit came out of his mouth.

The door opening quietly startled him. Around the corner Sophia appeared. She was wearing a pair of cute teddy bear pajamas as she walked toward him.

"What are you doing here?" he asked. The blanket she'd given him was wrapped around his shoulders. When she sat down on the mattress he was taken aback. Wasn't she afraid he'd hurt her?

"I couldn't sleep, and I needed to see you. Today was harsh."

Lash had forced him to fight back. The fact he couldn't get his body to move scared him. He'd been taking drugs for only a few months, but it was only recently that those drugs had taken effect. Thinking about his response he wondered how addicts who'd been taking for years were able to stop. He was having a hard time as it was.

Edward knew this wasn't him. Each challenge his brother set him, put him on course for recovery. Not being able to defend himself while being hit at by his own brother had angered him. There was a time when no one could get a hit past him, and now he was helpless. When Lash had pulled in close and forced him to look at Sophia, the bruises on her face, his brother made it clear that it was Edward's fault.

Nash wouldn't have let any man think he could hurt Sophia. Edward was different. This side of him was weak. It was helping him to make sense in a weird kind of way of how he'd let his life be controlled by something else.

"My brother has always been a bastard and always will. There's no stopping him from getting what he wants."

"Don't you want this?" she asked.

"I don't know what I want."

She reached over taking his hand. He stared down at the tattoos covering his arms. Each tattoo symbolized his part within the club.

You're nothing without the club.

Fight this and win. Be yourself again.

Sophia ran her fingers over each line of ink. "I remember when you got this. Kate was in the shower, and you showed me your ink. You were so happy to be where you were. I remember asking you why you loved The Skulls. Do you remember what you said?"

"The Skulls were a family. There was no judging. The family accepted you for who you were."

"And you said that you were never alone again. The club gave you a big family with plenty of brothers and sisters."

He recalled it all. The drugs, the addiction could take it all away from him. Edward knew he couldn't let that happen.

She held his hand within her own. Her hold was tight. He felt happy and secure from being held.

"Why are you even helping me?" he asked.

"I kicked you out of my apartment, and it was the biggest mistake I could have made. I'm to blame for this, and I'm going to do everything I can to make it right." Tears were glistening in her eyes. "I loved every second of that kiss, Edward. I haven't been able to stop thinking about it."

Staring down at their hands Edward wanted to cry, to scream at the lost time.

"Why are you telling me this now?"

"I need you to kick this habit. If you don't get rid of the addiction and become Nash once again it will kill you." She wiped under her eyes. "I want the man who helped me move. Who kissed me the way you did. I want him back. Not this."

He wanted to give it to her. Edward wanted so badly to give her everything she desired.

"Kiss me," he said.

She didn't hesitate at his instructions. Sophia closed the distance between them, pressing her body against his. He wrapped his arms around her waist, feeling her lush curves. Her ass was lovely and plump, and he gripped her hard. She gasped, banding her arms around his neck.

"This is real, Edward. This is what I want." She pressed her lips to his. Her lips were trembling and unsure as they caressed his own. Moaning, he reached up with one hand sinking his fingers into her hair and holding her tight against him. He despised the shaking and the sick feeling in his gut.

Her fingers clutched at the hair at the nape of his neck. Her legs circled his waist, pressing her hot pussy against him.

They moaned. The sounds of their kiss echoed off the walls. He wanted to drown in her scent.

Only when they heard movement did they break apart. Sophia stayed in his lap staring into his eyes.

"What does this mean?" Edward asked.

"It means that you fight this. You kick the habit. Give me back my man, and I'll be yours if you want me, Nash."

The sound of his name made his heart soar.

She cupped his face. "You can do this. I love you. I want you. Give me him back." Sophia kissed him again and extracted herself from his hold.

"This is not a trap or a joke?"

"No. I'm not like that, and you should know that." She kissed his lips again and moved away. "I needed you to know that before tomorrow."

"Has Lash got something worse planned for tomorrow?" Edward asked. His cock was rock hard. He'd not wanted sex in such a long time.

"Tiny is coming tomorrow. It's going to be a long day for everyone." She turned and walked away.

You should be following her. She shouldn't be walking into that room alone.

Lying down on the bed, he looked up at the ceiling. All he needed to do was fight. Fight this addiction, earn his place back in the club, and get his woman back.

Edward made it a mantra inside himself. There was something for him to fight for. It wasn't going to be easy. He wasn't stupid. He knew in his heart he'd have to fight with every part of himself to get what he wanted.

Tiny was coming tomorrow, and he needed to make the leader of The Skulls realize that he wasn't going to give up, not ever. Sophia had given him something to fight for, her.

****

Tiny sat at his desk in the club thinking about the following day. The last time he'd seen Edward, Lash had given him the update on what he planned, and he'd almost killed the son of a bitch.

The bastard had set off a gun and almost killed Eva. Closing his eyes, he tried to focus on the sheets of paper that Alex had left behind. He couldn't make out any of the numbers. The clubhouse was quiet, which was unusual. Most days the club was bursting with activity. Since Edward had gone no one was in the partying mood. The threat to The Skulls was higher than ever before, and all of them knew it was because of one of their own. Edward hadn't broken down in private, no, he'd done it so rumor could drift to their enemies, and Tiny had many enemies. He hoped most of them were not even close by to know the damage that could be done.

"Are you plotting and scheming again?" Eva asked.

He glanced up to see the other bane of his existence stood in the doorway. She was wearing a silk robe, but he'd snuck upon her early to see her wearing a sheer baby doll negligee. Staring at her, he felt the stirring in his groin. None of the sweet-butts were able to satisfy his cravings anymore. The only woman he wanted beneath him was stood looking at him with her arms folded. Since that night in Vegas he hadn't been able to get her out of his mind. According to her, he'd been completely shit in the sack. Had he grown complacent with the other women he'd been with?

"I've got to go sort out Edward tomorrow." He gritted his teeth. Saying his name aloud made it hard for him to cope. The boy was such a fucking disappointment and a danger. Eva walked farther into the room.

"So?"

"He almost killed you, Eva. I can't let that fucker in my club again."

"I'm not a member of your club, Tiny. I'm not an old lady or a sweet-butt. I'm nothing."

"You're not nothing, and you know it."

"Do I? Edward has been part of your life for a long time now, and you're just going to throw that all away because he made a mistake?"

"Don't fight for him. He's not worth it."

She threw her arms up in the air. "Why are you being so fucking difficult? Out of the twenty-nine years you've known him, he's let slip this once. How can you justify in hurting him?"

Tiny stood up. "Because he aimed for you." He walked around the desk, standing over her. She looked up at him, exposing the long length of his neck. "Any of the women and I wouldn't give a fuck about what he'd done. He risked hurting you, and that I can't accept."

Her expression softened. "I'm fine."

Pressing his hand to her chest, he felt her rapidly beating heart. "If he'd not missed he'd be dead by now, and so would Lash. I'd kill everyone who threatens you, Eva."

Tears were glistening in her eyes. Wrapping his arms around her waist, he breathed in her scent.

"I'm not that important, Tiny. You know it, and I do. Forgive him." She pulled away from him like she'd done so many times before.

He didn't know what to do to get her back. There were times he thought he was making progress, and then he'd slip up. When was he ever going to get what he wanted from her?

What *did* he want from her?

"I can't."

"Then you're not a very good leader." With those words hanging in the air, she turned on her heel and walked out of the door.

Watching her go, he went back to his desk and dropped his hand in his hands. Would he be forever cursed to screw up around her? Eva evoked feelings within him that terrified the life out of him. He wasn't ready to let her go. Tiny felt it was only a matter of time before she moved on, and he didn't have a choice.

NASH

Chapter Seven

Edward stared at the vomit on the floor. He heard Sophia running around trying to clear it up. Tiny was going to arrive any minute. Killer had moved him away from the vomit and soaped him down. He needed a bath badly. The stench of the last couple of days was starting to turn his stomach more than the withdrawal. His diet of porridge and water was starting to wear thin as well.

"Don't worry about the mess. I'll see to it. It's my job to make sure he's fine." Sophia pushed Killer out of the way. He watched the big guy take a seat and begin reading the newspaper. Edward didn't even know the other man could read. "How are you feeling?" Sophia asked, cupping his cheek.

Her touch made him burn from the inside out. Fuck he wanted to be inside her so bad. When he was well and sober he was going to spend a month fucking her hard. She'd like it rough.

"Like I've been run over by a fucking bus."

She smiled. "That's good."

"Me being in pain is good?"

"No, you being able to tell me that is good." She kissed his lips and wrinkled her nose. "You need to brush your teeth. You stink."

He laughed despite not wanting to.

"Get away from him," Tiny said, invading their moment. He tensed up, and Sophia tightened her grip on his face.

"It'll be okay." She got up, grabbing her stuff and leaving his side. Edward looked up to see the guy who'd beaten him badly. Tiny was fucking huge and scary. The scowl on his face gave evidence to his temper. Great, if Tiny got hold of him, he was fucked.

Tiny reached out grabbing Sophia's arm and drawing her in close. He heard her squeal and try to hide it. Tensing in the cuffs, he glared at where Tiny was holding his woman.

"What were you doing that close to him?" Tiny asked.

"He's been sick. I was cleaning him up." Her voice was small, but she didn't cower away from the man.

"I told you not to get too close," Lash said, speaking up.

"Someone had to clean him, and I didn't see the big lug giving me a hand. I did what I had to do." She tried to get Tiny to leave her alone. The leader of The Skulls kept his hand on her. "Let go."

"Get your hands off her," Edward said. He'd had enough of the power play.

"Are you talking to me, boy?"

"She's not your concern. Sophia is helping you, but that doesn't give you the right to be a dick toward her. I'm the one you've got a problem with. Me. I was the one who almost killed Eva. Deal with me."

Tiny let Sophia go. "You're right. My issue is with you."

The big man walked toward her. "Get these cuffs off him, Lash. He and I are going to have a little chat."

Swallowing past the lump in his throat, Edward stared past Tiny's shoulder to see the fear on her face.

"It's all right. Nothing is going to happen," he said.

Lash released the cuffs and helped him out of the room. He looked behind him as Sophia made to go to him. Killer held her back. His arm was across her chest stopping her from moving.

They didn't leave the building. He heard the doors being shut as they moved far away from the room with Sophia.

Tiny opened the far door on the right leading out to what looked like a gym. "Some of the boys have been using this place to make their own amusement. I thought it was rather inventive of them."

Edward didn't comment. It was the first time he was able to move around. Instead of using the time to his advantage he collapsed onto the floor sitting on his butt.

"Are you begging me for forgiveness?" Tiny asked.

"No, I know you better than to beg. You won't give me forgiveness until you feel that I've earned it." He was cold away from his blanket. Fuck, his life had gotten so messed up. "Are you going to finish what you started?"

"Am I going to kill you?"

"Yeah."

Tiny let out a sigh. Lash was stood near the far wall with his arms folded. "No, I'm not going to kill you."

The news surprised him. He expected the next time he saw Tiny he'd be dead within seconds. "If you're not here to kill me then what are you here for?"

"I needed to see you for myself. Lash has kept your space at the club. You're still a Skull."

"What about the votes? What do the guys think of an addict taking a spot?"

Tiny smirked. "They say the first sign of recovery is admitting you're wrong."

Looking down at his hands, Edward saw the muck and grime on him. "Yeah, well, I've had to see what my woman thinks of me like this. I never thought Sophia would ever be disgusted with me."

"Your woman opened your eyes."

Tears were fast filling his eyes. Edward was on rock bottom in a stink pit. "I remember my dad saying that the best men have the best woman beside them. I can't be by Sophia's side, and if she's prepared to give me a chance then I've got to get clean." She was his savior whether he liked the power it gave her or not. "This is not me."

He wiped the tears away. Edward was many things, but he wasn't a fucking pussy.

"Your father would be disappointed in you with this," Tiny said. "He'd probably take the belt to you, and so would your mom. They were good people."

Grinding his teeth together, Edward kept the tears locked in tight.

He would not cry.

Suddenly Tiny sighed. "I was coming here to kill you. Eva's mine, and you almost killed her, but you didn't." He sat down beside Edward. "The day your mom and dad died I kept my promise to always protect you, but the last few months I've been breaking that promise."

Lash looked as surprised as he felt.

"You're men, and as Eva said, you're twenty-nine years old and made one mistake. I've been neglecting my job as leader. It won't happen again. I'm not here to kick your ass."

Edward didn't say anything. He didn't want to risk upsetting Tiny.

"You earn your place back in the club, then it's yours. I'll back you, but you've got to get the drugs out of the deal."

"I'll do it."

"Good." Tiny slapped him on the back. "I've got to go and set a deal with Alex. The bastard is really starting to piss me off."

When they were alone, Lash sat beside him.

"You took a beating for me."

"Yep, and I'd take it again and again. You're my brother."

"Take me back to the chains. I can feel the hunger inside me to get a fix."

Lash helped him back to the main room. He saw Sophia stop mid-pace as they walked back to the room. "I was freaking out. He's not the kind of man you say no to."

Killer grunted.

"He's the boss, Sophia."

Collapsing to the bed he waited for Lash to put on the cuffs.

"Wait, what's going on?" Sophia asked.

"I'm going to finish this."

He felt weak. The determination was riding him hard. Edward wasn't going to let this be the end of him.

Keeping an eye on Sophia he forced himself to be okay with being locked in.

"We'll still keep an eye on you, and she won't be alone."

"Good."

She sat beside the mattress staring at him as Lash and Killer left the room. "What made you take the drugs?" she asked.

He repeated the story he'd told Lash. It was the truth, and he didn't see a point in hiding the truth.

"Was it me? Did I drive you to taking them because I was a fucking idiot and sent you away?"

"I was weak. I couldn't handle you pushing me away. Yes, I took them because of your rejection, you didn't push them on me. I was the weak one who couldn't say no."

"I didn't even know that Kate had the stuff. God, I was a bad sister."

"You were too damn good for her." He took her hand and held her tightly.

They were silent for a long time. Sophia broke the silence. "So you thought I was innocent?"

"Compared to me and the life I've led, you're innocent. You're not a virgin?"

Her cheeks went bright red. "No, I'm not a virgin."

"Neither am I."

She chuckled. "Let's not talk about the past. You were with Kate, and I was with a guy. We can move past that."

"A guy?"

"Edward, stop it." She looked at their hands.

Staring at her bowed head, he felt his heart explode with happiness. He knew all about the guy she was with, but he wasn't going to think about that. When he was with The Skulls, before he fucked up, he could have anything. The women and the booze all came to him along with the parties. The Skulls couldn't give him what he actually wanted, which was Sophia.

"I hate my name," he said, trying to distract himself.

"Then work hard and get Nash back."

"Do you think I can do it?" he asked, needing to know her thoughts.

"I think you can do anything that you put your mind to."
****

The week passed silently, and Sophia helped Edward throughout it all. The Skulls took turns helping out. She spent her days cooking, cleaning, and talking with Edward. The guys talked about club business, which she ignored. Lash stayed with them the most. When the guys were busy, she played cards with Edward on the mattress. She'd baked a chocolate fudge cake and stolen him a slice to enjoy. When the shivering and the vomiting ceased, Lash would take him out for a walk.

On those days Sophia stayed inside waiting for the men to get back. She was more thankful when Lash offered to take his brother for a bath. The stench radiating off Nash had made her feel sick at times. Zero stayed the most. She was a little afraid in case he'd started to have feelings for her. Sophia noticed that he would find any excuse to touch her.

"We're taking the restraints off for good today," Lash said on Friday night, the second week of staying in the factory. "Also, we've got some work to do, so it will only be you and Edward tonight."

"When do you think you'll be calling him Nash?" she asked.

"Soon. On Sunday a lot of the guys are going to be stopping by. We're going to make sure he's ready to join us."

"You're afraid if he'll fall off the wagon."

"It has been known to happen for addicts." Lash looked past her to a sleeping Edward. "He's going to be around booze, and he's got to get used to it."

They'd all agreed that Edward would be best off not drinking or taking anything that could risk him spiraling down.

"You're leaving me alone?" she asked.

"Edward would never hurt you, and I don't like the way Zero is around you. I'm going to bring some distance between you and the guys."

She nodded. "I'll take care of him."

Lash handed her the keys. "We're going to lock up the building, so no one will come inside. You'll be safe."

Sophia didn't say anything.

"Let him out when you're comfortable." He turned to leave. She watched him go, wishing he wasn't leaving her. At the door he stopped and glanced toward her. "Thank you for helping me. The Skulls will always offer you their protection."

The door closed, and she was alone with the man she loved with her whole heart.

"You don't have to let me out if you don't want," Edward said.

She turned toward him. Edward was sitting up against the wall. He was wearing clothes and looked more like the guy she first met than ever before.

"You were awake?"

"I'm a pretty light sleeper, babe. The drugs doped me enough to sleep throughout the night." He let out a yawn, which made her laugh. "Lash told me he was going to leave the decision up to you. I don't blame him. We're here alone, but he's right. I'll never hurt you."

"I didn't think you'd hurt me."

"I'm not offended." Edward stared at her. "I've been an ass to you."

"Do you remember everything you did with the drugs in your system?" she asked.

"Yeah, I knew what I was doing. I'm going to have to live with that for the rest of my life." He looked sad, and she hurt for him.

"I forgive you," she said. The keys felt heavy in her palm.

"You shouldn't forgive me. I was a fucking bastard, and you should be hating my guts."

"I've never been good at that." She tucked some hair behind her ear. The bruises from Gill and his friends had all but disappeared. The guys hadn't hit her that hard.

"I've missed you," he said, catching her by surprise.

"I've missed you, too. I never wanted you to go that day." She walked closer knowing she was to release him from the cuffs.

He stared up at her. Leaning over him she released one cuff then the other. Moving away, she put the keys down on the table and checked the chili she'd started to cook on the stove.

Out of the corner of her eye she saw him rubbing his wrists.

"Now that feels weird without the cuffs," he said.

"Do you feel like your old self?" she asked, tasting the chili. It was hot and spicy, just how Edward liked it.

He got up from the bed and made his way over to her. "I am my old self. What just happened feels like a fucking nightmare." His hands banded around her waist. She gasped, not used to his attention.

"Sorry, I just needed to hold you without being chained to a fucking wall." He buried his head against her neck, inhaling her scent.

"At least you don't stink," she said.

They both chuckled.

Letting go of the wooden spoon, she placed her hand on top of his. "I'm pleased you're not chained to a wall anymore." He tightened his hold on her. "Go to the table. I'll serve you up some chili."

He went without protest. Grabbing two bowls she served enough for each of them, then sprinkled the tops with cheese before heading toward the table with him.

She saw him take the first spoonful, and the look on his face filled her with confidence. "I take it you like my chili?"

"It's the best damn chili I've ever tasted."

Smiling, she ate her meal wondering what the hell to say. Whenever they were alone before when he was dating Kate, they talked all the time. Eating her food gave her a reason to be silent, but she knew it was only a matter of time before Edward said something.

"Lash is bringing the guys tomorrow. I'm going to get tested to make sure I'm strong enough to be in the club," he said.

"Is it going to be bad?"

"Yeah."

"Okay, what is it?"

"You have to prove your strength to remain within the club. I'm going to have to fight some of the guys to prove that I have a right to be part of The Skulls."

She dropped her spoon. "No, you can't fight anyone. You're just getting over … everything. I'm not going to let them hurt you."

He took her hand. "I haven't got a choice in this, baby. Being a Skull is my whole life. I can't turn this down. I don't fight then I'm out for good."

Swallowing past the lump in her throat, she picked up the tray and headed toward the sink. "What if they hurt you?" she asked. The thought of seeing him fight filled her with dread. There were still bruises over his body from what Tiny had done to him before. She understood why he got the beating, but this was not part of that.

"They'll hurt me, and I'll prove myself." He got up, standing close to her. Edward pushed the hair off her shoulder, exposing her neck.

Turning toward him, she stared up into his eyes. They were dark, penetrating eyes. Every time she looked into their depths she always felt drawn to him.

"I don't know if I can handle you getting hurt."

"You're a strong woman. Sophia, you can handle this." He cupped her cheeks, keeping her focus on him.

"I'll handle it," she said after some moments passed.

"Good." His fingers caressed across her lips. She gasped from the electricity his touch created.

They were alone. No one was coming into the building, and Edward wasn't chained to a wall.

Heat flooded her pussy as his thumb pressed between her lips. Staring into his eyes, she opened her mouth, accepting him inside. She heard him gasp, and then he was walking her backwards.

She hit the wall, and he crowded in front of her. He took her hands pressing them against the wall. She dropped her gaze to his lips.

"I want you, Sophia," he said.

Biting her lip, she forced herself to look into his eyes. "I want you, too."

His mouth was on her within seconds. There was nothing gentle about the possession of his lips. Edward plunged his tongue in deep as he held her hands above her head. Their fingers were locked together. His cock was brandished against her pussy, pressing the thickness of him into her.

Edward broke the kiss going to her neck and nibbling down to where her pulse had to be beating rapidly.

Her heart was racing and her pussy dripping wet. He always made her feel this way around him. It was like the man she'd known for a long time was finally back in her life. Pulling his hands away from hers, both palms lay on her chest, holding her steady. "If you don't want this, you've got to tell me to stop," he said.

"Why wouldn't I want this?" she asked.

She'd denied herself once before, and she'd almost lost him. Sophia didn't care what he said. The only reason he took the drugs in the first place was because she pushed him away.

There was no way she was going to make the same mistake again.

"Are you sure?"

Taking hold of his ears, she slammed her lips on his. "Do you doubt me now?"

He tore at the shirt she wore. She tried to help him tug the shirt over her head. They were moving fast. With her shirt on the floor, she started working on his clothing as he effortlessly got her naked.

This was going to be their first time naked together. She worked at his jeans until they were stood only in their underwear. The black boxers did nothing to obscure the view of his rock hard cock pressing against the front.

"I'm at a disadvantage," he said, pushing the straps of her bra down her shoulders. His fingers slipped between the clasp at the front.

There really was no turning back now.

****

"The Skulls need to come to an end," Rick slammed his fist on the table making the glasses rattle. "They've ruled long enough. It's time someone else takes the lead."

Gill listened to his friend, liking the idea more and more of taking over the biker club that ruled the town where he lived. He was sick and tired of living with the threat of the club. Fort Wills was not a town to be controlled. The only other problem he had was the fact he'd lied to cover up the reason they were doing the recon on the club. His and Willy's job was to know what The Skulls were up to for another biker group. He'd lied to everyone in this room, and if the men found out the truth, he was fucked.

"Do you think you can take over? Create fear and have The Skulls quaking in their boots?" Gill asked. He needed to instill fear, as otherwise he was going to be dead at the hands of a biker from Darkness. *Shit, I've really fucked up this time.* Three men had taken them on a couple of weeks ago, and they were all still trying to recover. He said as much to the group of ten men. All of them were vicious criminals wanting a place to make their own. He'd been scoping the box factory out to see if it was safe to start making their move on behalf of his employer.

He'd lived on the outskirts of Fort Wills most of his life. The town was everything he needed, small, quaint, and prepared to have a force that wasn't the law take over. When he'd been contacted over a month ago to rally together a bunch of men for a mission to watch The Skulls, Gill had been excited. He'd not told the men what the real plans were. If the men in the room knew he was using them, Gill knew he'd be dead within seconds.

"We can take them on. They're weak," Rick said. He'd murdered multiple women in his time on the road. Gill had a lot of respect for the man. He respected anyone who was going to take the law into their own hands.

"They're not weak, and anyone who thinks they are, is insane," Bishop said.

Glancing around at the convicts in his midst, Gill smiled. "They're all weak. Edward Myers has them all divided. A lot of the men won't want a druggie in their club. A club divided is a club weakened."

"You look like you've got a plan, Gill. Let's hear it."

"The men are weak when it comes to their bitches. They put a shit lot of protection on them."

"You think going after the bitches will weaken them?" Rick asked.

He shook his head. "No. Attack two of the women, and they'll put all the protection on them. No one watching their back will give us the opening we need. I know where they're staying and when to hit out. These men will not see it coming."

Gill had been contacted a few hours ago by Scars. Their next point of attack was the women. He needed to get control of these men before they found out the truth. Once the others had done their job, he knew the members of Darkness were going to take them out. So long as he played his part, he'd have a chance of living.

Get the job done, and live through it.

All of the criminals nodded and smiled at his suggestion. It wasn't his suggestion, but they didn't need to know that. They settled around the table and began plotting the demise of The Skulls, which was really the plan he'd been ordered to complete.

Chapter Eight

Flicking open the clasp, Edward stared at the full round globes of her tits. Fuck she was well stacked, and his mouth watered. He wanted a taste of her ripe flesh. Licking his lips, he dipped down, taking one of her red tipped nipples between his teeth and sucking on it.

Her head fell back against the wall, gasping for breath. She sank her fingers into his hair, pulling on the strands. Edward refused to let up, sucking on her hard.

"Please, harder," she said, moaning.

Biting down on her large nipple he gripped the edge of her panties and tore them from her body. Releasing her body, he rid himself of the boxers he was wearing.

Edward let go of her breast and took a step back.

"What are you doing?"

"I'm admiring, baby. Fuck, you're so damn beautiful." Cupping his cock, he rubbed his length needing something to release the tension building inside him. She looked so fucking sexy. He wanted inside her, but right now he'd explode at the merest provocation.

"You never had a woman before, Edward?" Her hands lifted against the wall, thrusting her breasts up high.

Some men wouldn't like the extra flesh or the curves she possessed. He couldn't wait to get hold of those curves and make her his.

Reaching out, he stroked a hand from her stomach up to her breast. He fingered the hard nub pointing up at him. "What are you waiting for?" she asked.

"What's your rush?" He'd gladly spend the whole night simply touching her.

"This is my rush." She took hold of his hand and slid it between her thighs.

Stroking through her wet heat, Edward almost lost it. She was dripping wet, soaking his fingers with her cream.

Her pubic hair was nicely trimmed giving him perfect access to her pussy. Sliding his fingers through her wet slit, he teased her clit, feeling how hot and swollen she was.

She whimpered. Her hands went flat to the wall behind her.

He sucked his cream covered fingers, tasting her. Sophia's eyes widened as she looked at him.

"How do I taste?" she asked.

"Like heaven."

When she went to her knees, he lost all thought. Sinking his hands into her black hair, he bunched the length in his fist as she gripped his cock. He never thought she'd be like this. Edward always assumed she would be shy and he'd have to take the lead with everything. She was knocking the wind out of his sails with her actions.

He knew she wasn't all that experienced. There was a clumsiness to her movements, but still, he wasn't going to complain.

She fisted the length, gazing up at him through drooping eyes. "What would you like me to do?" she asked.

"Take me into your mouth," he said.

Sophia opened her lips for him to see before going back to his shaft. He watched as he licked the tip. His foreskin was pulled back with the strength of his arousal. The top leaked small amounts of pre-cum, enough to coat the tip.

Her moans had him reaching out to hold onto the wall.

He'd never known such noises could turn him on. One of her hands gripped the base of his shaft while her other rested on his leg. Her tiny fingers sank her nails into his flesh.

In that moment Edward realized he'd almost lost this. He'd almost lost his woman for some fucking high. This was the biggest high he needed. Being around Sophia provided him with enough happiness that he didn't need the shit he inhaled into his body.

"Fucking bastard," Edward said, yelling the words as she took the entire tip of his shaft into her mouth. He'd gotten his dick sucked plenty of times by the women who visited the bar or the sweet-butts, but none of them had ever left him feeling like this.

Sophia was enjoying what she was doing. The other women were simply performing an act that was expected of them. He saw the difference and understood more than ever why his brother and Murphy were happy to settle down. Their women loved them. Tate and Angel wanted to make their men happy and would do anything for them.

He wanted Sophia. The desire to make her happy swelled within him. The hand at the base of his cock started stroking up and down as her head bobbed down to meet her hand. Her tongue stroked him even as her mouth sucked him in.

Staring down he saw her eyes were closed, as she worked his dick.

After several seconds of sucking him, she pulled away, opening her eyes and looking up at him. It took sheer willpower not to explode into her mouth.

"Am I doing it right?"

"I'm hanging on by a thread, babe. You've got no idea how good your mouth feels on me." He stroked her cheek, pressing his thumb between her lips for her to suck on.

She gripped his hips and pressed him against the wall. "I want to do this. I think you deserve a little pleasure."

With his back to the wall, she gripped his shaft and went back to licking him. Her tongue caressed over the entire length, coating him with her saliva before taking him back into her mouth.

Wrapping both of his hands in her hair, he tightened his grip, needing to do something with his hands. It was only a matter of time before he completely lost control. The grip he had in her hair helped him to set the pace of her movements. He thrust up into her mouth and held back. Edward didn't want her to be scared of him if he went too deep, choking her.

She cupped his balls in her free hand, stroking them. It was too much. The pleasure of her tongue and the feel of her on his balls was all it took to send him over the edge. He didn't have time to warn her as he plundered her mouth going as deep as he dared and releasing his cum. Sophia swallowed him down. Her hands went to his thighs, holding onto him.

His grip tightened harder in her hair as the orgasm put him to his toes.

"Fuck." He yelled the words to the rooftops. She didn't release him until she'd swallowed every last drop of his cum.

Opening his eyes that had closed through his orgasm, he stared down at her. Sophia was staring at the floor, her hands in her lap as she waited for him.

Letting go of her hair, he cupped her cheek, forcing her to look at him. Her eyes were dilated and her nipples rock hard. What she'd just done had turned her on, and in knowing that, Edward felt an answering arousal build inside him.

"That was amazing," he said. Out of all the words he knew, amazing didn't even begin to describe what she'd done to him. He went down to his knees, staring into her eyes and showing her the love he felt for her.

She cupped his face between her hands. He heard her chuckle, nervously. "I've been wanting to do that to you for a long time."

He looked at her. "You've fantasized about being with me?" Her head jerked in answer. "What else have you fantasized about?"

"I'm not telling you tonight." Her hands stroked over his lips. He loved the feel of her touch on him. Dropping his head down, he claimed her lips, not caring that he tasted himself on her tongue.

"We've got all the time in the world." Getting back to his knees, he took her hand and led her back to the mattress he'd been sleeping on. Lash had gotten rid of the other one he'd been sleeping on. There was no way he was using one he'd vomited near and sweated in. Fortunately, his brother hadn't argued with him.

Sophia had been on his side for a new bed. He couldn't leave this building until the club accepted him back into the fold. Edward needed to earn back his place to become Nash once again.

Once he earned his place back, he was never going to risk fucking it up.

"Lie down. Open your thighs."

"Edward, what are you doing?"

The chains were still against the wall, and the keys were on the table. "Having a little fun. Trust me."

She lay down on her back. Her eyes never once left his.

Taking hold of one of her hands, he gripped the cuff and sealed it around her wrist. Edward did the same with the other one.

Her breathing deepened, and her eyes went wide. "You're not going to leave me here, are you?"

Stroking the side of her face, Edward shook his head. "I've got you bound to the bed where I can do whatever I want to you. I'm not letting you go, and I'm certainly not walking away from this."

Running his fingertips down from her face, he circled the bud of her nipples. "You're open for me." Down his fingers went, circling her belly button before going to where his prize lay. Her legs were wide open like he'd asked her to be. "I get to worship your body with no one interrupting. This is our night together. The first night of many and there's no way I'm letting you shut me out."

He dipped down to her pussy, caressing the outer lips of her sex. Her cream had soaked through.

"How long has it been since you last had sex?" he asked.

"A long time ago."

"When?" He felt jealousy clawing at him. If Zero had touched her, he'd fucking kill his fellow brother. Screw the club. Sophia was more important than some club.

"The night I lost my virginity was the last time I had sex. It was crap, and I didn't want to repeat it."

Edward paused in caressing her. "You've only had sex once?"

She nodded. "Are you going to laugh at me?"

He shook his head. "Hell no. I'm going to be the last man you're ever with." Edward was also going to make sure she remembered the experience for years to come.

****

Sophia nibbled her lip. Edward was looking at her as if she was something to eat. She tested the cuffs that bound her to the mattress. Was she a fool for letting him do this to her? Probably. She'd never been tied in place with no choice but to submit to the man in front of her.

Two fingers thrust inside her making her cry out. He moaned. "You're wet."

She'd not been with anyone in over two years. Losing her virginity at eighteen had been a mistake, but this was not. She was already hotter than hell for the man fingering her pussy. A third finger was thrust inside her, and Sophia gasped as he turned and began stroking across her g-spot. The pleasure was intense and unlike anything she'd ever felt.

All too soon he withdrew his fingers and sucked them in his mouth. She'd never seen anything more erotic than the look of pleasure on his face every time he tasted her.

She watched him settle between her thighs. His flaccid cock was getting hard once again. His hands went to either side of her head, and she looked up at him.

"Keep your focus on me." He leaned down, claiming her lips. Edward didn't ask for permission; he took what he wanted. She gave it to him, opening her lips so he could explore her mouth.

She moaned, wanting to feel more of him all at the same time. His lips moved from hers going down to her neck. Sophia cried out, struggling against the cuffs. Edward had moved the mattress far enough away so she couldn't fight the restraints. She was helpless against his onslaught.

"I've got you right where I want you," he said, teasing a nipple. Glancing down she saw him circle her nipple with his tongue before biting down on the red bud.

Staring up at the ceiling she cried out, whimpering with need. "Your body is so responsive, Sophia."

He moved to the other nipple and gave it the same attention. From his touch to her breasts she was losing control. The desire to close her legs to find any contact to her clit was intense.

Edward stopped it all. His big body stopped her from getting the sensation she wanted.

Crying out, she screamed for him to give her a release.

"When I'm good and ready, baby."

She'd never heard him torment her sister and told him as much.

"Don't bring Kate into this, and I never cared about her. With you, I want you screaming, begging me for more." His teeth bit down making her arch up against his touch.

Only when he was satisfied with her response did he move down. He went down her stomach, lavishing every part of her front with his tongue.

Closing her eyes, she tensed and tried to pull out of the cuffs.

Note to self, never let Edward and cuffs near me again.

Collapsing to the bed, she kept her eyes closed and waited for him to finish torturing her.

He eased down between her thighs. His fingers opened the lips of her sex. "What are you doing?" she asked, tensing.

"I'm giving you the same kind of pleasure you gave me." His tongue attacked her clit, flicking the nub.

No matter how hard she tried, Sophia couldn't contain her screams. The pleasure of his tongue was too much.

She felt his fingers opening her sex wide as he sucked her clit into his mouth. Her cream was leaking out of her cunt and dribbling down to coat her anus.

Sophia stilled as his tongue left her clit, going down and plunging inside her. Looking up, she saw his hands had moved to grab her hips. He fucked his tongue inside her. It was the weirdest feeling in the world, but the pleasure was amazing.

After several strokes of his tongue, he went back to her clit as his fingers took over.

She tensed up as one finger penetrated her pussy and the other stroked against her ass.

"Relax, baby. I won't do anything you don't like," he said.

Slowly, she relaxed every muscle she could think of in her body. She didn't have much choice but to wait for him to do what he wanted to do with her. Part of her was excited by his ministrations while another part was scared. What if she didn't like it and couldn't satisfy him? What if she liked it too much and disgusted him?

A quick grinding years ago from a guy hadn't set her on course for a good comparison. He'd not even given her an orgasm that she could recall.

Edward added a second finger, opening her wider.

"I'm a big man as you know. I don't want you to be hurt when I fuck you." He muttered the words against her clit. She understood what he was saying. It was probably the first time in her life she'd been considered too small for anything.

Any other time she'd have laughed at what he said. Edward chose that moment to push the tip of one finger against her ass. She clawed at the blanket underneath her needing something to hold onto through all the pleasure he was causing her.

He tongued her clit as he fucked her pussy and explored her ass. She'd never known anything like it. Sure, she'd read saucy books when she was alone, but nothing ever described this kind of pleasure or possession. Edward was taking her on a rollercoaster ride of sensation, and she didn't know if she'd ever survive it. He was working her body as if he alone knew how to bring the ultimate response from her.

"Come for me, baby."

Without her even realizing it, she'd been thrusting up to meet him, stroke for stroke.

"I can't," she said.

"Yes, you can, Sophia. I'm here to catch you, baby. Let it go." He sucked her clit hard, and Sophia saw stars as something exploded inside her. Her stomach tightened, and her body tensed as pleasure shattered her apart. She moaned, giving herself over to whatever he was doing to her body. Sophia didn't want him to stop.

Edward kept licking her throughout her orgasm. Finally, when she could stand it no longer, he kissed her clit and eased up toward her. He took possession of her lips. Sophia tasted herself on his tongue. She kissed him anyway, not repulsed by her own taste.

"We're even," he said.

She frowned. "What do you mean?"

"I've made it my mission to guarantee that when I find release, you'll find release." He took her lips once again. "And, Sophia, I intend to always be one orgasm in front of you."

Laughing, she tried to wrap her arms around him but was stuck. "I can't move."

Edward left her side, grabbing the keys from the table. He released her, and together they snuggled down on the mattress.

His arms held her tight, and Sophia never wanted him to let go.

"How are you feeling?" she asked. The last couple of weeks crashed around her, reminding her of why she was in the building with him.

"I'm fine. I feel like an asshole to be honest. The guys are always going to be nervous around me. I've got to show them and prove to them I'm strong." His hands ran up and down her back.

"You're never going to leave the club, are you?" She looked up at him. Her head was resting on his chest. One of his arms was around her back as the other was behind his head. He looked down at her.

"Do you want me to leave the club?"

She thought about what Lash had said. The club was everything to Edward. Losing it would lose part of himself. Not to mention all the enemies he'd made doing jobs for the club.

Did she really want him to leave the club? It had made him the man he was, the man she'd fallen in love with. She didn't want him to change.

"I don't want you to leave the club. I like you just the way you are. Obviously, without the coke head. I didn't like you then." His hand gripped her arm tightly.

"I said some pretty fucked up shit to you that day."

She reached up, stroking his face. "Don't worry about it."

"I'll never forget the hurt on your face at what I said. I'm so sorry."

Tears filled her eyes, and she blinked them away. She was done with crying. Over the last year she'd done a lot of crying, both when Kate was alive and when she died.

"It's in the past. You weren't the right man then, and you're not going to fall back to being like him either." She followed the outline of the skull tattoo on his chest. "And I won't let you fall back either. Lash is the same. We're here for you."

His hand moved down to cup her ass. His fingers slid through the seam, caressing over her anus. She tensed up, gasping.

"I'm not going to lie to you, Sophia, the urge is there. Lash told me a few days ago that the detox is never the problem. His plan was risky, and it could have killed me. The biggest problem an addict faces is the need for it."

"Do you still feel the need for it?" She should get points for being able to talk. His hands were doing wicked things to her body, making her melt once again.

"Yeah. I feel the need for it, but I don't want to fall down again. I've got too much to lose, and I know you'll walk if I take again."

She wanted to dispute him, but Sophia knew in her heart that if he started using again, she wouldn't be able to handle it. His mood swings, the nastiness came with it. She wouldn't be able to survive it again.

"I'll be here every step of the way. I'm not going anywhere." Sophia had nowhere else to go.

The man she loved was right in her arms, and the club he was with offered her protection. She'd never had a problem with The Skulls. Glancing down his body she saw he was rock hard once again.

Chapter Nine

The night was disappearing fast, and Edward didn't want to lose a moment of it. After tomorrow he didn't know if he'd be able to be with her for a couple of weeks. His brothers were not going to be easy on him, even if he asked them to. He wouldn't dare ask them to go easy on him for sex. His love for Sophia would last far longer than the next two weeks.

Sex could wait. Having Sophia in his life could not.

"What are you thinking about?" he asked, knowing the direction of her thoughts.

Her gaze returned to his. Her cheeks were flushed, and she stumbled over her words.

"Is my woman thinking dirty thoughts?" he asked.

The color of her cheeks got even deeper. She nodded, and her lips stayed shut.

Smiling, he rolled her onto her back. Sophia opened her thighs for him, and he settled between them. Leaning down, he claimed her lips, seeking for her to open to him. She opened her lips, and he plundered inside. Their moans mingled.

Their kiss was passionate and drove him wild. His cock hardened even more, and he was desperate to be inside her.

Rearing back, he broke the kiss and stared down at her. "If you don't want this to go any further then you need to say so now."

"I want this."

"Be sure. Once I'm inside you I'm not going to stop."

"I'm sure, Edward. This is what I want." She sat up, wrapping her arm around his neck and bringing him down to kiss. "I want this more than anything."

Pushing her back to the bed, he gripped his length and eased the tip through her creamy slit. She was still wet, and he coated his cock in her cream.

When he bumped her clit, she jolted, chuckling as she did. "I wasn't expecting that."

"You're sensitive."

She nodded.

Pressing the tip to her cunt, he pushed inside so only the head was inside her. "Then how does this feel?" He gripped her hips and plunged inside her.

Sophia cried out, arching her back as he hit the hilt deep. The walls of her sex clung to him. He felt every ripple of her pussy through the one thrust. Edward stayed seated inside her, not moving.

Slowly, she opened her eyes and stared up at him. He saw her swallow.

"Are you ready for me to move?"

"Yes." Pulling out of her tight heat, he glanced down to see his cock coated with her juices. Before he pulled all of the way out of her, he slammed back inside. It felt like he was going deeper with each thrust. Over and over again he pulled out of her only to slam deep inside her. He didn't let up. The pleasure was too intense for him to simply stay still. Her hands gripped his forearms, her nails sinking into his flesh causing a biting of pain.

"Edward, slow down," she said.

He caught her words but couldn't stop. Opening his eyes, he saw the pleading look she was sending him. Gritting his teeth, Edward forced himself to slow down and to give her what she wanted. He stopped, pausing deep inside her.

Shaking, he focused on her. She let go of him panting for breath.

"What's the matter?" he asked. "Am I hurting you?"

"I'm not used to it. Can you take it slow just this once? It's too much for me."

Nodding, he settled down around her. Pushing the hairs off her face, he kissed her lips. "I can slow down for now."

His body was shaking from the need to fuck her hard. All of his life he'd fucked hard. Never once had he taken his time with a woman. He took deep breaths trying to slow himself down.

She caressed his back, going down to cup his ass.

Pulling out of her tight cunt, he made each move as slow as he could go, drawing out their pleasure. Sophia was tight, tighter than any pussy he'd ever been inside. She was also drowning him with her cum. Not only was she the tightest pussy he had, she was the wettest, and he fucking loved it.

Kissing down her neck, he sucked on her flesh. She writhed underneath him, thrusting up to meet him.

It didn't take Edward long to love the slow pace of making love to her. He felt every ripple and relished every cry of pleasure. Making love slowly gave him the chance to catch every reaction his dick caused.

"This is it now, babe. You've got me for the rest of your life." Slipping a hand underneath her knee, he raised up, pulling her legs over his shoulders. Gripping the flesh, he glanced down watching his cock slide into her cunt. "Watch us together."

She looked down at where they were joined as one.

The inner walls of her sex gripped him tighter. "That's it, Sophia, come on my cock. Let me feel it."

He slipped a finger between her silken folds and caressed her nub. Within seconds she splintered apart around him. He didn't know how he was ever going to last with the flutters of her pussy around his dick.

127

Her cries lost him completely.

Gripping her hips he fucked her hard, pounding inside her. He didn't let up, and he realized she wasn't pushing him away. Sophia was holding him tightly as he rammed into her over and over again.

"I can't slow down," he said. "I need you too fucking bad."

"I don't want you to slow down." Her voice sounded breathless. A sheen of sweat coated her skin.

Leaning down he plundered her mouth in the same way his cock was plundering her cunt. She met him thrust for thrust.

He felt the stirrings of his orgasm in his balls. Edward kept thrusting inside her. Three deep thrusts and the first of his orgasm claimed him. Grunting from the power of the pleasure he spilled his release into her waiting pussy, flooding her with his seed.

The only sounds to be heard in the room were their rapid breaths. Collapsing on top of her, Edward cushioned his head on her full breasts.

She wrapped her arms around him.

His head was buzzing. He'd just made love to the woman he loved. The fact he wasn't wearing a condom didn't bother him. If she got pregnant he'd deal with it.

Rolling over her eased her onto his chest.

"I'm too heavy." She tried to push away, but he wouldn't let her.

Holding her in place, he kept his cock inside her. "You're not going anywhere. We just fucked, and now we're going to cuddle." One of his firm rules was never to cuddle. He was breaking that rule for her. Also, he wanted to cuddle with her. Edward wanted to bask in the afterglow of their lovemaking.

"I'm sorry for telling you to slow down," she said, easing her head against his chest.

"This is your second time having sex. I loved taking my time." He stroked her back, needing to touch every inch of her skin.

"I'm sure you're not used to women asking you to slow down. I don't imagine Kate ever—"

There was no way he was letting her finish that statement. Slapping her ass, he jerked her chin up to face him. "Don't even fucking compare yourself to your sister. You're nothing alike, and I'm not going to be comparing performance."

Taking hold of her hand he pressed it against his chest. "You're here, Sophia. It's about more than sex and fucking. You mean far more to me than getting a fuck. I can get a fuck from any willing woman. You're different."

He saw her swallow and nod. "Okay, Edward, I get it."

"You're not someone I'm going to let go of. You're not a sweet-butt. I'm keeping you."

She smiled. "I'm not some kind of possession. I'm a person with feelings."

"Feelings for me, Sophia. I know you love me."

"It's not attractive you being like that," she said.

Chuckling, he squeezed her ass. "I don't care. I've not forgotten about the men who hurt you either. They'll pay for what they did to you."

"Forget about them, Edward. They're not worth it. We're together." She dropped her head.

"I'm not forgetting about the bastards who dared to hurt you. I wouldn't be a good Skull if I left them unpunished." He kissed the top of her head.

"You're not the law."

"In this town I am."

She looked up at him, resting her chin on her hands. "Don't get yourself hurt."

"I won't. I'll earn back the guys' trust, and then I'll take them out. None of the guys like men who can't respect the word no."

She rested her head back on his chest. "Am I going to wake up and all this be a dream?"

"I hope not. This is the best I've ever felt in my life. When I wake up I want it to be the same." Holding her tightly, Edward finally allowed himself to relax and rest.

****

"Well, isn't this a sight to wake up to," Zero said.

Sophia moaned, feeling Edward underneath her. Why was she hearing Zero's voice? Last night had been wonderful. She couldn't remember a time when she'd been so happy. Throughout the night Edward had made love to her, taking her to new heights of pleasure and back.

"What the fuck, Zero?" Edward said.

Opening her eyes she became aware of the gazes falling on her and Edward. She'd fallen asleep on his chest last night after he'd taken her for the third time. Wincing, Sophia became aware of the soreness of her body. Turning her head she saw several of The Skulls staring down at them. Yelping, she tried to cover herself with the blanket. In trying to cover more of herself, she ended up pushing the blanket off her entirely.

Edward fixed her dilemma but not before his club got an eyeful of her body.

Sinking her head onto his chest, she covered her eyes.

"I see you used last night wisely," Lash said.

She kept her head covered not wanting to see the smirking or the disgust on their faces.

"You could have knocked or given us a warning," Edward said.

"Please, my father is not the one to be kept waiting. Besides, you should know him," Tate said.

At the sound of the female's voice, Sophia chanced a glance to see Tiny's daughter carrying a tray. "I came with coffees for me and Sophia. It's time I got to know the woman in his life."

She heard Edward moan. "One morning with you and she'll run away from me."

Tate glared. "Shut it, you."

Glancing around the room, Sophia saw the men were no longer gawking at her, apart from Zero, who looked like he hadn't dropped his gaze.

"Will you guys fuck off so my woman can get dressed without you looking at her?" Edward asked.

"You're not trying to get out of the beating you're about to get, are you?" Butch asked.

"No. I'm going to earn my place again, but when I'm back to being a Skull I'll be keeping Sophia as my old lady."

The silence in the room was deafening. She wanted the floor to open up and swallow her.

"Sophia will always be protected. She's an old lady now, but you've still got to earn your spot," Tiny said. "Come on, men. Give them some privacy."

One by one the men filed out leaving her alone with her man. "My God, that was so embarrassing."

"Guys, I'm still here," Tate said.

Sophia jerked toward the small kitchen area where Tate was working the stove. "You can have your cuddly feelings later on. I'm working on my skills to woo the latest woman in our club."

Edward gripped her ass. "I've got to get ready, baby," he said.

He eased out of the bed, grabbing his shorts before standing up. She checked his ass out, and then he was moving toward the bathroom. Wrapping her body with the bed sheet Sophia approached the table.

"Hi, I'm Sophia," she said, introducing herself to the other woman.

"I know who you are. I'm Tate. Tiny's daughter and Murphy's old lady."

Sophia shook hands with the other woman.

"It's nice to finally meet you. I'd heard about you from the guys who were here the last couple of weeks. You earned their respect, and that's hard to do unless you spread your legs for them." Tate handed her a coffee. "It's the good stuff. I can never make it like the shop downtown does."

Sipping at the coffee, Sophia took a seat at the table. The blanket covered her modestly.

"So, you're the latest addition to the club. Angel and the others are going to love you. Is your hair natural or out of a jar?"

Sophia took a giant gulp of coffee staring at the woman before her.

"It's natural."

"You're not very talkative."

Smiling, Sophia lifted the coffee. "I need a lot of caffeine to get me wired."

"Good, my kind of girl. The others will be joining us soon. The girls wouldn't miss Edward earning back his Nash title. Especially after the shit he pulled at the diner. Angel's special day and he fucked it up big style."

She listened to Tate prattle on. Edward left the bathroom ten minutes later looking refreshed and ready for the day. Getting up from her chair, she made to pass him. He caught her elbow and pulled her in close. "I loved last night."

"Me, too." She pressed her head against his. The outer door opened letting in all the men.

"Today I don't want you to interfere. What you're going to see is tough, but it'll be worth it." Nodding, she pulled away, heading toward the bathroom.

Staring at her reflection she saw three marks from his lips. She blushed remembering the way he'd sucked on her neck.

Dropping the blanket she checked out the other marks he'd left on her. Toward the end of the night, he'd become a very passionate lover. He sure liked to play rough, and last night he'd given her a taste of everything he liked.

Well, actually, with the way he kept playing with her ass, she didn't imagine he'd shown her *everything* he liked. The guy might have an ass fetish.

Climbing into the shower she let out a gasp at the coldness of the water. The bastard had used all the hot water. She washed, dressed, and was back in the room with the rest of the men in no time.

Tate was dishing out breakfast to each of the men.

"You didn't leave any hot water," she said, crossing her arms over her chest.

"Yeah, sorry about that." He patted his knee for her to sit down.

"If Murphy didn't leave me any hot water he wouldn't be able to sit down for a month. I'd kick his ass that bad."

Sophia laughed. She looked at the big man and couldn't imagine Tate hurting him. All of the bikers looked like forces to be reckoned with. Their cuts displayed their part in The Skulls.

The other woman handed her a plate. Sophia took the plate and sat on Edward's knee to eat. He caressed her leg going between her thighs. She slapped his hand. "You didn't leave any hot water. I'm not in the mood to play."

Tate chuckled, clucking her tongue at Edward.

Sophia ate breakfast, every now and then slapping his hand away. Sophia didn't care about the hot water, but she liked the way he kept trying to touch her regardless of it. Once breakfast was finished she helped Tate with the dishes. The men were talking about everything. Sophia couldn't keep up, but Tate joined in without looking phased.

"You'll get used to it in no time," Tate said.

When the dishes were done Edward took her hand pulling her out of the room, deeper into the building. They entered a room that looked like a gym. There were mats on the floor. Angel, Eva, and a couple of other young looking men with the word "prospect" on their jacket were standing there.

"Baby," Lash said, opening his arms.

Sophia watched as the blonde woman threw herself in Lash's arms. "I missed you."

"Are you going to be able to handle this?" Lash asked.

The fact Edward's brother was asking that question unnerved Sophia. "You've gone all tense," Edward said.

"I'm nervous." She watched all the men removing their cuts and cracking their knuckles. "Isn't this a little childish?" She felt the panic rising up inside her. They were all being immature, and she didn't like the idea of Edward being hurt. She'd only just got the man back. Yes, two weeks wasn't that long, but Lash explained everything to her about the progress of getting his brother drug free.

He cupped her face. "If you had a choice to have a man who you knew could defend you no matter what the cost or a man you had to take his word on defending you, who would you chose?"

"That question makes no sense. I don't need protection." Edward wouldn't let go of her face as she struggled to pull away.

"Stop it. It's important. These men are my family. If I can't fight them and they're the hardest men I know, then how the hell can I call myself a Skull?"

She stopped fighting him, hating the fact he was right.

"I love you, baby. Nothing is ever going to change that, but I need to prove that I've got their back. Not only that, I've got to prove they can trust me." He pressed his head to hers. "I know you're going to hate this. I haven't got a choice."

"It's time," Lash said, invading the moment. Glancing behind her she saw the women were set up on what looked like bleachers at a high school. "The women love to watch."

Sophia doubted it. The women were sticking around to make sure the men were not hurt.

"Let me do this."

"Fine."

He still wouldn't let her go. "I love you." Edward took possession of her lips. The feel of him brought the memories of the previous night came flooding back to her.

"I love you, too."

"Come on, pussy," Zero said.

Pulling away she sent Edward a smile before taking a seat between Angel and Tate.

"Everyone, I want to introduce you to Edward's-slash-Nash's, woman, Sophia." Tate made the introductions. "That's Angel, Eva, Sandy, Rose, Kelsey, and the two fuckers on the end are the new prospects. Their job is taking care of us and doing the mundane shit."

Sophia smiled at everyone before returning her gaze to the main floor.

"I hate this more than the parties," Angel said. "At least in the parties I know he's going to be okay."

"We're all worried. My babe is going to beat the shit out of him," Tate said.

Sophia winced as the fighting started. She didn't recognize all the men, but Tate pointed out them all. Killer was currently throwing some punches at Edward. She pressed her hands over her eyes not being able to watch.

"Kick him in the balls," Sandy said, screaming out. "I love it when men fight. They look all sweaty, and I'm getting horny."

Sophia wished she could get horny instead of wincing every few minutes. The men were relentless in their attack.

Chapter Ten

Four hours later the guys backed away. Edward was standing on his feet but barely. Tiny and Lash hit the hardest out of all of the men. He didn't know if they were going to let him back in the club. The one person he was having an issue with was Zero. The other man kept eyeing up his woman. Not that he blamed him. Sophia was the complete opposite of the club, and yet she fit right in. She was wearing a pair of blue jeans with a red and black checkered shirt. The top few buttons were open revealing an expanse of creamy cleavage. Zero was using every opportunity to look at her.

"Sandy, come and check him out," Tiny said.

The blonde doctor came rushing down to check his war wounds. He stayed still staring at Sophia. His woman looked worried. Edward nodded his head for her to come down. She walked down, tucking some of her black hair behind her ear.

Zero helped her down from the bleachers, lingering a little too long for Edward's taste. Grinding his teeth he stayed still as Sandy poked and prodded him. He jerked when she prodded at his ribs.

Sophia chuckled at whatever Zero whispered against her ear. Didn't she realize he was copping a feel of her behind? The bastard knew what he was doing, and it was driving Edward mad. When he got his title back Zero wouldn't be mauling his woman.

She pulled away from Zero going straight for him. "Is it over?"

"You stayed away like I asked." Opening his arms, he waited for her to step closer. Sophia hesitated. "What's up?"

"I don't want to get in her way. She needs space to treat you." She nibbled on her lip.

"Come here anyway. Sandy doesn't mind."

"No, I don't. Hug him. He deserves it." Sandy smiled up nodding her head. He'd gladly kiss the doctor for giving his woman permission to come close to him.

"Please tell me it's over." She kissed his neck.

Glancing toward Tiny he waited for the other man to give his consent. Tiny jerked his head. "Yeah, it's over."

She wrapped her arms around his neck. "I couldn't have watched much more. You must be hurting all over."

"I ache, but I'm alive. I did better than I thought possible."

Sophia grasped the back of his head and smashed her lips against his.

That's right, Zero. She's fucking mine.

Turning away from Sandy he held his woman.

"Enough, enough. Alex needs us back at the clubhouse. You're staying here, Edward. We'll let you know if you're a member of the club," Tiny said, heading out.

Jerking away from his woman he watched as the boys left the gym one by one. The women were leaving as well. They all pulled Sophia into a hug. His brother and Angel stayed behind.

"What the fuck, Lash? I did everything you asked. I took the fucking beating. What gives?" Edward had fully intended to be a member.

"Shit is hitting the fan out there. Two weeks is a long time in club business. We've not been able to do our run, and some of our buyers are hitting out." Lash took a step closer leaving Angel a few steps behind. Edward knew his brother didn't bring his woman into club business. He couldn't keep shit from Sophia.

"The guys think you're responsible for making us look weak." Lash was whispering to him. "News spread about what happened at the diner and then at the club. We're in a delicate position right now. Tiny's thinking of calling in Chaos Bleeds."

Pulling back Edward looked at his brother. "He's not fucking serious." If people thought The Skulls were rough, they hadn't met the other biker club they knew. Chaos Bleeds were a rough bunch of thugs. They were not like The Lions that they'd taken down over a year ago. Chaos Bleeds really didn't give a fuck about rules or sticking to one place. Over five years ago they'd breezed through town only stopping long enough to have a good time. Tiny had made friends with the leader, Devil.

Edward didn't like them. If the other biker group were to come to town then Fort Wills was looking at a pretty rough couple of months. "I'm not getting back into the club, am I?"

"You are. Tiny just has business on his mind. Eva's father is not happy either, and he's making waves to get her back to Vegas. Alex is intervening. We need you, brother. You chose the wrong fucking year to have a breakdown." Lash put his hand on Edward's shoulder.

"I need this, Lash. Don't leave me out in the dark." He hated begging, but if he had to beg and literally kiss Tiny's ass then he'd do it. Edward didn't have just himself to think about. Sophia was his woman, and he needed to protect her.

"It's the rules, brother. I wish you were there as well. At the moment, you're not part of club business. You are the business." Lash slapped him on the shoulder.

"Talk to Tiny. Chaos Bleeds is not the answer for us."

"They're friends, Edward. They're our only answer if the rumors circulating are true."

Grinding his teeth, Edward did his best to keep his opinions in check.

"What is it?" Lash asked.

"Nothing."

His brother gave him a pointed look. "I've seen you do that look many times before. You've got something on your mind, so spit it out."

Sophia ran her fingers up and down his chest, calming him.

"Tell him what's troubling you."

"If Chaos Bleeds comes to town then we're not going to look strong at all. People will know that we can't control our town. If Tiny brings them in, then he needs to make sure no one knows why."

Lash nodded. "I'll tell him. I'm sure he hasn't considered that."

His brother slapped him on the shoulder and went back to Angel. Edward watched them all go wishing he was taking Sophia with him back to the clubhouse. Crap, he'd have to get a place for them. He wouldn't be able to handle her little apartment.

"You're still tense. Come on, we'll get you cleaned up," Sophia said.

He followed her through to the area of the factory where they'd been staying.

"I'm curious about this place. Why are there a kitchen, bathroom, and living quarters?" Sophia asked, distracting him.

Edward chuckled. "This was the staff quarters of the food factory. Some of the guys converted this to suit their needs. We've always had plans for this place, but nothing has come of it."

She helped him remove his clothing. Glancing down at his body he saw the bruises from the jabs the guys had gotten in. "Give me a number on a scale of one to ten, ten being the worst and one being not so bad. How does my face look?" A couple of the guys had gotten a few punches to the face.

"About an eight."

He cursed. "I take it there will be no kisses for me?" he asked.

Sophia chuckled. "You just got your ass kicked and you're more concerned about being kissed?"

"I'm an optimist. Kiss me, baby. Make it all better."

Edward was sat on a chair in the makeshift bathroom with his woman stood between his legs. He ran his fingers up and down her thighs, wanting to feel her bare flesh against him.

She leaned down and gently brushed her lips against his. He didn't want gentle. Edward wanted hard and rough. Reaching around her head, he pulled her tighter against him, ignoring the pain.

"You'll hurt yourself."

"I don't care. Kiss me, baby." He moved down going to the button of her jeans. When he'd walked into the gym prepared to take his beating he'd put sex to the back of his mind. Right now, his cock was rock hard, and the only person who could satisfy the craving deep inside him was standing between his thighs.

"We can't," she said, trying to pull away.

"We can."

"You're hurt."

"Not enough to *not* want you." He took hold of her hand pressing her palm against his rock hard cock. "See, I want you."

She rolled her eyes. "You're always hard."

Sophia removed his clothing until he was stood before her naked.

"Take your jeans off."

"Edward, be serious."

"If you don't want me to fuck you then fine. If you do, then take your fucking jeans off and get to your knees."

Her eyes widened, and her cheeks were a deep red. She loved being bossed around, and Edward was more than happy to do that. Her hands were shaking as she unbuttoned her jeans and started to push them down her thighs.

Kneeling down before her, he pushed the jeans the last of the way. His patience was fast running out.

"Come on, Sophia. I need inside your cunt."

"You're too fucking crass."

He slapped her ass, getting turned on by her cussing. She yelped but didn't move away. Sophia went to her knees before him. Her lush ass faced him. Opening her knees slightly, he ran his fingers through her tight wet slit. His woman was dripping wet and ready for him.

He'd never grow tired of her sweetness.

"Edward, don't tease me," she said. Her voice sounded breathless.

"Are you feeling needy?" he asked.

"You know I am."

"Then tell me to fuck you hard."

He heard her growl, and the sound make him chuckle.

"Fuck me, Edward."

Gripping his cock, he ran the tip through her cream, coating his shaft. He bumped her clit with the tip of his dick.

She cried out, trying to push back against him. Edward held her in place with a grip on her hips.

"I'm not letting you go. I'm in charge, Sophia. Stop trying to take over." He slapped her ass, and he loved the red of his hand print on her pale flesh. She was never going sunbathing on his watch. He loved the paleness of her skin. The marks he put on her would always be visible to him and to the world.

"Stop hitting me," she said.

He guided his cock to her core and slammed deep inside. She screamed but didn't fight him. "I'm spanking you, babe." He slapped her ass again.

Her cunt rippled around his shaft. His love taps were turning her on.

"Stop it," she said.

"No, I'm not stopping anything. I feel how turned on you are. Stop fighting it."

"It's not right." She moaned as he reached around to finger her nub.

"Don't give a fuck about what's right or not. I care about what feels good. Go with it. Don't fight it."

She moaned, slamming back against him.

"Take your shirt off. I want you naked."

Her head rested on the floor as her hands worked the shirt. He reached around to stroke her clit as she got naked for him.

Once she was completely naked, he caressed her breasts and pinched her nipples. She cried out, and her pussy was squeezing the life out of him.

"Fuck, yeah, baby, fuck my dick."

****

Sophia never thought she'd feel like this with another person. Edward was making her explode with sensation, and she didn't want to hide from what he evoked within her. His grip returned to her hips, squeezing the flesh.

"I'm going to spend all night fucking you, and when I'm done you're going to want me all over again."

She didn't dispute him as he pounded inside her. His cock touched every inch of her inner walls drawing her closer than ever before to orgasm.

"Please, fuck me," she said, begging him.

"That's it, take my cock."

He was very vocal as he grunted with each slamming thrust. She felt him so deep that the pleasure was on the verge of pain. His hands moved to her shoulders, and his thrusts were harder than ever before.

Screaming, Edward hurtled her into a mind blowing climax. Only his hold on her shoulders kept her stable and safe away from any hard floors.

"Fuck, yeah. I can feel you tightening around my dick. Fuck, you feel so good." He slapped her thigh and ass. The pain from the sting drove the pleasure even deeper.

She couldn't take much more, and suddenly he tensed. Sophia felt him release inside her. The pleasure took her breath away.

Where he held her shoulders, she knew there would be bruises. His grip was that tight. Slowly he lowered her to the floor with him following her.

"I can't believe I'm laid on a bathroom floor," she said.

"We'll be washed soon, and then I'm riding you back to bed."

She giggled. Her muscles were sore, and she didn't want to move from her space. "I can't move."

"I'll do all the work."

And Edward did. He carried her into the shower, which surprised her with her added weight. She didn't comment though. Their past together had taught her not to talk about her figure. Edward seemed to love it, and she wasn't going to say anything that could damage their time together.

After they finished in the shower, Edward carried her back to bed. It wasn't quite dark, but Sophia couldn't think of anywhere else she'd rather be than in his arms.

They lay down on the mattress, and she ran her hand up and down his arm. His back was to the wall, and she was sat between them. "Do you ever miss Kate?" she asked.

"No."

"Sometimes I do."

"She was a bitch to you, baby. I know she was still your sister, so don't start bitching at me."

Laughing, Sophia turned to look up at him. "I used to get jealous of her when she brought you home. I hated hearing you two together."

His arms banded around her.

"Don't think about her. I forbid you to."

"And I've got to listen to everything you say?" she asked, teasing him.

"You got that right. I was thinking when I'm patched back in we can go house hunting," he said, taking her by surprise.

"House hunting?"

"Yeah, we're going to need a place bigger than your apartment, and I've only ever really lived in the clubhouse. I doubt you'll be wanting to wake up every morning with the guys padding around." She didn't dispute him. "We've got to get our own place, and it has got to be big enough for our kids."

"Kids?" Didn't he realize how he sounded? He was talking about stuff she'd not been thinking about.

Been having sex without a condom. What do you expect to happen?

She'd not given it a thought. Pressing her hand over his where it lay against her stomach she felt herself gasp.

"Are you only realizing that you could be pregnant right this minute?" he asked, nuzzling her neck.

She went with honesty. "I hadn't been thinking about it."

"I've done nothing but think about it."

Needing to see his eyes, she pulled out of his grasp and turned full to see him. When she was with him, Sophia wasn't conscious of her nakedness.

"You've really been thinking about it?" she asked, catching his face in her hands.

"Yeah, I have." His palms settled on her ass. "I want to have kids. I can't wait to see your stomach swollen with my son or daughter. Not to mention how big your tits are going to get."

She felt his cock swell against her. An answering pulse settled between her thighs.

"Does it bother you?" he asked.

"No. I'm hot all over thinking about having a family with you." She claimed his lips, pressing her breasts to his chest.

"I'm going to get fucked now, aren't I?"

Sophia straddled his waist and took hold of his length. She aligned them both up together before starting to ease down onto him. He wasn't completely hard, and she was able to seat herself on him without it hurting.

They were both moaning by the time she returned her hands to around his neck. Edward caressed her ass, stroking along the seam.

"You've got a thing about my ass, don't you?" she asked.

"When all this shit is over and behind us, I'm going to fuck you in the ass. It can be my treat."

She gasped, feeling arousal spin through her. Anal sex was something she'd read about in books.

"You want to have anal sex with me?"

He started chuckling.

"Baby, I want to fuck your ass. I can't describe anything so hot as clinically as you do. Your ass is mine."

She felt his fingers push against the seam of her ass. Tensing in his arms, she was shocked as his cock swelled even more inside her.

"You're hot at the thought of me being inside you."

Sophia stuck her tongue out. "You'll be my first."

"You know what to say to drive me crazy." He kissed her deeply while also raising her up and off his cock. With the tip of him inside her, he slammed her down going so deep she had to hold onto his shoulders. "Now it's my turn to drive you crazy."

He jerked his hips up, and Sophia wrapped her legs around his waist. She tore at his mouth, plunging her tongue inside and stroking along his own. Sophia felt all the walls she'd kept around her shatter. Her love for Edward was complete. She'd follow him no matter what. Her feelings for him meant far more than the protection the club offered her. To her, Edward had always been part of her life even when he was dating Kate.

He wasn't dating her.

Edward was going to give her so much more. He wanted a house and a family. For a long time Sophia had given up on the dream of having a family. She was in her early twenties, and she didn't want the responsibility of raising children. When it was only she and Kate it had been difficult for her. Having no parents to take care of them had made it hard for her to think of being part of a family. Kate was out most of the time leaving her to handle the bills and cooking.

"Come back to me, Sophia," Edward said.

She hadn't even realized her eyes were closed or that she'd stopped moving. His cock pulsed inside her, but he'd stopped thrusting inside her.

He cupped her cheek. "Where did you go?"

"I want to have a family with you." She stared into his eyes. "I can't think of anything more amazing. I want to make a baby. I want it all."

She hoped she wasn't scaring him with what she wanted out of life.

Edward pushed the hair off her face. "Baby, if you're not pregnant now then I'm making it my mission in life to get you so. I'll be on you all day every day until we have a little stick telling me we succeeded."

"I love you."

"And I love you. Never doubt it, but now I want you to fuck my dick." To make his point, he gripped her hips, pulling her off his shaft and plunging her back down on him. Sophia cried out. The pleasure that had dimmed through her panic was now back claiming her.

She rode his cock hard, taking him as deep as he would go.

"Yes, harder, baby." He slapped her ass again, and the pain brought her closer to orgasm. "Touch yourself," he said.

Reaching down between them, she started to finger her pussy, touching her clit. Edward took over and helped her to ride him. He was rock hard, and every now and then he kissed her lips.

"Come for me," he said, ordering her.

She focused on her clit, stroking herself. Within seconds she cried out, her orgasm catching up to her.

Edward squeezed her ass, rolled over so she was underneath him, and then slammed in deep.

He took over, ramming inside her with such force that he took her breath away. His relentless thrusts sent her over the edge into another orgasm.

"I'm going to make you come again."

She didn't think it was possible, but he proved her wrong by sending her over the edge once again. Edward was the one in control. He fucked her hard, touching her in ways that made her feel special.

Only when he was ready did he let himself find release. She felt him jerk within her, his cum soaking her womb, making her think of babies and the future. When his orgasm started to ebb away, he wrapped his arms around her and held her close.

"I love you so much. We're going to have a baby, and nothing is going to stop us getting what we want."

His arms wrapped around her. Sophia felt safe, protected in the sanctuary of his arms. She could face the world with him by her side.

"You're going to get your spot back in the club, Nash."

He tensed. "Don't call me that until we know."

NASH

Chapter Eleven

The following day he was getting testy. He fucking hated being cooped up in the abandoned factory while his fellow brothers, the club he ran with, were dealing with shit on the outside. Sophia was sat in a long denim dress watching him pace.

"You're going to get tired walking up and down like that."

"I can't help it. My boys are out there." Resting his hands behind his head, he walked toward the door and backed away. He was grounded to this place. There was nowhere else he could go, as otherwise he'd put the rest of the crew in danger. He understood the risks, but right at that moment he couldn't think of a better way of spending his time than finding out what happened.

Walking over to Sophia, he lifted her wrist into the air to read the time on the watch. It was a little after twelve. He'd eaten porridge and drunk fucking coffee. Now he was raving to go, and he was nervous about the results of yesterday.

What if the reason they were staying away was because they no longer wanted him? Crap, he couldn't handle this.

"This is why Lash is keeping you out," Sophia said, rising from her chair.

"What?"

"You're not in control right now. The guy, the addict, he's in control."

"They need me, Sophia. I can't sit around and wait for them."

"Yes, you can, and you're going to do exactly that, or so help me, I will chain your ass back to the wall." She poked at his chest, her glare making him shut up.

"I need to help them."

"Then help. Get better and do as you're fucking told for them. You fucked up once. Don't give them another reason for you not to be part of The Skulls." Her hand rested to his chest. "Be in control. Be Nash."

Nodding, he wrapped his arms around her. His whole body was tense and on edge. This was the longest he'd ever been kept waiting for anything in his life. The only other person he'd waited for was Sophia, and now she was his. He was going to do everything in his power to keep her. Edward was sure of one thing, and that was his love for Sophia.

He hoped by the end of the day he was back to calling himself Nash. Edward was such a pussy fucking name. No one was scared of Edward Myers, but Nash had a reputation all of its own.

Two more hours went by with not a word. Sophia distracted him as best she could by playing cards or touching him. Nothing was going to distract him. Every single one of The Skulls had a decision to make.

Just wait. Everything will be fine as long as you wait.

Taking deep breaths didn't help, and neither did pacing. Sophia stopped helping and watched him in between making coffee. For fun she started telling him where to walk. Even when he didn't want to, he found himself laughing.

The laughter was short lived as the door was opened. Lash and Murphy walked through the door. The looks on their face sent a shot of fear up his spine.

"What's going on?" he asked.

"Our enemies are inside Fort Wills. We don't know who they are, but Tiny's contacted Devil. Chaos Bleeds is on their way," Lash said.

Murphy was white as a ghost. Looking between the two men, Edward knew they were keeping something from him. "What's going on?"

"Whoever our enemies are, they went after our women."

"What?" Sophia asked. She moved to stand beside him. The Skulls never hit at women or civilians. They followed their own code of how to handle things.

"Tate is in hospital. She was rundown by a car with no license plate. There were witnesses, but everything is fuzzy."

"Is Tate going to be all right?" Edward asked. Murphy still hadn't said anything.

"They discovered she was pregnant, but she and the baby are doing okay even from the trauma. The doctors have warned it could still go either way," Lash said.

"That's not all, is it?" Sophia asked.

"Eva was attacked in a supermarket and is in a coma. Kelsey was shot in the arm, and Sandy was stabbed on her way to work this morning. They seem like completely random events, but they all have one thing in common ... us." Lash slammed his hand down on the table. "I've put Angel into lockdown. I think it's time you do the same."

"I'm not known to be around The Skulls. I'm running out of clothes, and I need to get to my apartment. It has been a couple of weeks," Sophia said.

"No, you're going to lockdown," Edward said. Their women had been targeted. "The only women who haven't been hit are the ones that had a Skull on them?"

"Yes. Tate was leaving the Salon when she was hit," Murphy said. "I didn't even think to put a prospect on her ass. She was so excited about Nash coming back and Sophia being with them. I'm so fucking stupid."

Sophia caught his arm, forcing him to turn and face her. "You need to help your brothers. You can't be worrying about me when they're the most important."

"You're not going home." He was not willing to risk her life. Sophia was the only reason he'd fought so hard with the detox. If he lost her, he'd go back to using to find that high he always got around her.

"I know it's not appropriate, but we were going to come and tell you today that you're patched back in. Everyone was amazed by your detox. Your strength has come through, and we all need you right now," Lash said. He handed over the leather jacket he was holding. "Tiny got you another one made, and he apologized for the damage he caused. He wanted me to let you know he shouldn't have gone off on you like he did. You deserved the beating, but not for the reason he gave it to you. Tiny wants to make sure everything is okay between the two of you."

"Of course. I was a fucking dick." Edward was shocked by the jacket. No, he wasn't Edward anymore. He was Nash. He'd earned his patch once again, and there was no way he was losing his patch again. Running his hands over the leather jacket he felt complete. This was everything he ever wanted.

Looking up at the two men, he put the jacket on his shoulders.

"It's good to have you back, brother," Lash said, embracing him. Murphy slapped him on the shoulder, and he turned to Sophia.

She ran her hands up the front of the jacket. "You look sexy, Nash," she said.

He was back and ready to fight for his club.

"It's time to go to the clubhouse. The club needs you." Lash left the room, leaving the door open wide for his freedom.

"Are you ready to come home with me?" Nash asked.

Sophia was smiling. "You were so worried they wouldn't want you back."

"I'm never going to give them a chance to regret this," he said.

"They won't." She disappeared into the spare bedroom, and she came back with her case.

"I'm not taking you home." He took the case from her and headed out. Lash and Murphy hadn't come on their bikes. They were in a truck. Helping Sophia into the back, he climbed in beside her and slammed the back of the door shut.

Nash put his arms around his woman, holding her close. She rested her head against him. Her hands were freezing cold, but he looked out of the window wanting to be up to speed with everything.

"Do we have any leads?" Nash asked.

"No. Tiny thinks it's the drug lord's family who attacked us last year. We can't confirm it. Killer doesn't think it's The Lions. He believes his old club wouldn't go quietly about taking over," Murphy said.

"What if it's independent?" Sophia asked, speaking up.

Lash was driving, but Murphy turned to stare at her.

"What?" All three men barked the word out in unison.

Sophia held her hands up. "None of you have a clue who is responsible for attacking you. I just think it's a little foolish ruling everyone out that you already know.

Why not think outside of the box? Maybe it's a threat you're not used to. Someone who has been watching and waiting."

Nash saw that she had a point. The last few months had been a little hazy with the drug taking. He was out of the loop on a lot of things.

"Look, we'll get to the clubhouse, and then you can fill Tiny in on all the crap when we get there. He's freaking out with Tate and Eva down," Lash said. "No, he's not freaking out. He's livid. He wants the bastards to be put down."

Holding on tight to his woman, Nash couldn't even think about anything happening to her. The very thought of visiting her in the hospital made him feel sick.

"Nothing is going to happen to me," she said. "I'm not going anywhere."

The drive was a long one. The factory where he'd been staying was on the outskirts of town in the very opposite direction from the clubhouse.

When sitting in the back of the truck there were no windows to see out of. He stared at the blank metal wall, wishing there was something he could do or remember to help. An unknown enemy was the worst type of enemy. Without knowing who had the problem, they were stuck on what to do or where to turn.

The Skulls were a force to be reckoned with. Only a fucking idiot would take them on and think they could get away with it.

"Look out!" Murphy yelled.

Tensing, Nash turned to look as the truck was crashed into from the side. He was thrown forward with Sophia doing the same. Nash couldn't hold onto her and watched, helplessly, as she slammed into the other side of the truck hitting her head.

"Fuckers! Lash, watch out."

Another hit sent him into Sophia. He heard something break and didn't know if it was him, Sophia, or the fucking truck.

The tires were blown out, and the final jolt shoved the truck over. There was nothing for him and Sophia to hold onto. They were going with the truck with no source of help. He hoped his brother had his seatbelt on as they kept rolling over.

The truck stopped, rocking upside down.

Coughing, Nash felt something sticking in his arm. Glancing down, he saw some wire and pulled it out, crying out as he did. The doors to the truck were opened, and men in masks charged in. Before he could get up and fight he was pulled to his feet.

"Remember, they're needed alive," a male voice said. It was the only thing Nash heard.

Something stuck in his neck, and all he could hear was Lash's voice. What terrified him the most wasn't his brother's voice. It was the fact Sophia hadn't said a word. She wasn't even moving.

****

"Nash!" Lash shouted for his brother through the pain and fog. He couldn't make sense of anything other than the fact his brother was being taken. When he saw Sophia being lifted he heard the sniggering from the men. Coughing, he fought the seatbelt that held him. Murphy was groaning at his side.

At the sound of the truck that had knocked them over, Lash lost it. He started to tear at the seat belt containing him. He needed to get out of the fucking truck and get to his brother before anything happened to him.

"Lash, calm down," Murphy said, groaning. "Fuck, I hate being in truck accidents. I prefer my fucking bike."

"They took my fucking brother." Reaching into his pocket he grabbed his cell phone. Forcing himself to act, he typed in the club's number, tapping his fingers on the steering wheel. The windscreen had broken, and glass was all around them. He was sure a couple of shards were embedded in his face.

"Hello," Angel said, picking up on the fifth ring.

"Baby, I need you to put Tiny on the phone. Now." She didn't argue and did exactly as he asked.

"If that was Tate she'd have my ass for speaking to her like that," Murphy said.

"I know. That's why I'm married to Angel."

He heard the commotion over the line and waited for Tiny.

"What the fuck is this, Angel? I've not got time for fucking phone calls." When he saw Angel and got the chance to, he was going to give her the time of her life to make up for the way Tiny had just spoken to her.

"It's Lash. It sounds urgent."

"This better be fucking urgent, Lash," Tiny said, speaking down the line.

"Get Angel away from the phone. Tell her to go cook or something." Lash waited for Tiny to give out the order.

"What's going on?" Tiny asked.

"I'm currently upside down in the truck. Your seat belts work a charm. I can't get fucking out."

Silence met his statement. "What the hell is going on?"

"Long story short, trucks just rammed us off the road, blew out the tires, and whoever they are have kidnapped my brother and Sophia. Murphy and I are stuck. We need help getting out."

Tiny was hitting something.

"Killer and Zero are on their way with the tow truck. Chaos Bleeds are just arriving. Get here quick."

The call disconnected, and Lash slumped down in his seat. This was the last thing he wanted to deal with today.

"Do you think Sophia was just coincidence, or do you think they were after her?" Murphy asked.

"I don't fucking know. They were after Nash. We know that. I heard one of them say he needed to stay alive. All I know is that I need to get the fuck out of here and get to my brother. Anyone who fucks with him could send him spiraling down. I can't let that happen."
****

Every part of her body ached. There was not a part of her that didn't hurt. Sophia moaned, pressing her hands to her head only to be stopped as her arms were jerked back. Opening her eyes, she groaned again from the pain. Her head was hurting so bad it was making her feel sick.

"Does she make this much noise when she fucks?"

Frowning, Sophia turned her head in the direction of the noise. She couldn't bring herself to open her eyes as the pain was too much.

"Fuck off." Nash's voice forced her to open her eyes. Shooting pain unlike anything she ever felt made her close them again. She'd not got a clear visual of everything that was happening.

The sound of flesh hitting flesh met her ears. She winced as Nash's cry of pain reached her as well.

Open your eyes, Sophia. Open them.

Slowly, she looked through slits. The room where they were was light, too light. Looking up, she saw the roof was made of windows, casting the sun down on them. Doors were swung open, and that was when she realized they were in an abandoned warehouse. There were a lot of them around Fort Wills after the recession. The nearest warehouse not owned by The Skulls in Fort Wills was about twenty miles south of the town. The warehouse had been abandoned for years. She heard rumors that a lot of the kids came here to fuck rather than do anything else.

"I bet she's a fucking rock star in the sack. A big woman like that needs to be able to put out. Why would anyone stay with her otherwise?"

She didn't recognize the voice. Nash's voice was the only thing she recognized.

"You're a fucking dead man if you hurt her."

Laughter followed his statement. Someone yanked on her hair, sending electric bolts of pain through her system. Tears stung her eyes, and she tried to follow the action of the guy holding her hair. The pain was unbearable.

"I'm hurting her, bastard. By the end of the night I'm going to be hurting her in ways that will make you cringe. Gill wants her for himself, but his orders are to keep him alive."

The foul odor of his breath made her feel sick. Leaning over, she threw up everything she'd eaten at breakfast time. None of the man's words made sense. Who wanted Nash alive?

"This whore is nasty. I don't know why anyone keeps her around."

The men were talking thick and fast. She couldn't make out a single word. When she dared to open her eyes, she turned toward Nash. He was sat in a chair with armrests on either side of him. A belt was wrapped around the middle, and rope held his wrists and legs into place.

She hated the sight of him tied down and wished there was something else she could do to help him. He was looking at her. His eyes widened when he saw she was awake.

"We're going outside for a smoke. Don't try anything stupid." The guy tugged on Nash's hair before shoving him.

Sophia didn't recognize any of the men.

"I thought you were dead," Nash said, catching her attention. Opening her eyes, she turned toward him.

"Why are we in a warehouse? What is it with guys and warehouses?" she asked.

"I don't know about this place. At least we know who the men are or at least what they look like."

"Are they friends of yours?" She lifted her hand and stopped. There was a metal cuff wrapped around her wrist halting her movements. She was chained to a table in the center of a warehouse. *Don't go panicking any time soon.*

"No, they're not friends of mine or the club. What is the last thing you remember?" he asked.

She focused on her last memories. Sophia saw herself in her mind's eye. Nash had his arms wrapped around her, and then the truck jerked. She recalled slamming against the opposite side and then nothing. Everything that happened was a blur. After telling Nash, she waited for him to say something.

"The hit must have knocked you out cold. They hit us a few times before we went rolling."

"We rolled?"

"Yeah. Lash was okay. He was shouting me as we left the car. The bastards injected me with something though. Fucking knocked me out cold," Nash said. "We're going to get out of this."

Even through the pain, she started to laugh.

"Why are you laughing?" he asked.

"We're stranded in the middle of nowhere. You're tied to a chair, and I'm strapped to a table with guys we don't know as our captors. I don't think we're getting out of this one easily." She felt the tears spring to her eyes.

"Aw, baby, don't cry."

Sophia tensed as she recognized that voice. Turning her head she saw Willy and Gill standing together. Her ex-boss and tormentor looked a little too cozy for her tastes. When she saw what they were carrying fear took over every part of her body.

"Do you know these men?" Nash asked.

She nodded, not wanting to look away from the threat in the room. The pouch they were carrying looked scary. She'd seen movies where men had brought out similar looking pouches, and no one left the room alive or in one piece.

"Sophia here owes us a little something," Gill said, moving toward her. "She's ours, but you're here for collection. We'll get our money then."

Tensing her whole body, she felt the tears spill out of her eyes as he got closer. Gill wasn't making any sense, but she'd never understood what he had to say. His hand reached out, touching her stomach and curving up to fondle her breast. Every muscle in her body protested, and the pain sensors fired in her brain, but Sophia screamed.

"Get your fucking hands off her." Nash tugged on the rope. She saw him fighting to get free. She smiled at him, trying to encourage him to break out of the bonds.

Nothing was happening.

"Gill, leave her alone. We're not here for that, yet. We've got to wait until *they* get here. I'm not willing to risk my ass until business is over." Willy slapped the other man's hand away. "We've got a lot more surprises up our sleeves before then."

"I hope to God it's a sock puppet. They're the only things I'm fucking afraid of," Nash said.

Closing her eyes, she wanted to beg him to be silent and to shut the fuck up. These men were fucking dangerous. She'd sensed it about them from the first moment she met them.

"He's fucking hilarious," Willy said.

"Don't be fooled by him, Willy. The bastard passes a mean punch." A third guy had joined the room. Sophia glanced over, not recognizing him. He was carrying a bag himself, and she saw Nash tense up.

"I take it you know him," Sophia asked.

"Of course he does. He doesn't know my name. I'm his supplier. The supplier he beat up. Do you remember me, Nash?"

The whole warehouse grew tense, or at least she and Nash grew tense. Something was telling her that they were taken for something more than killing. Their day was about to get a lot harder.

NASH

Chapter Twelve

Lash watched as Devil stood inside The Skulls' compound. The leader of Chaos Bleeds looked threatening as he glared around him. Tiny was stood facing the other man waiting.

"When I got your call I was expecting some reunion of some kind. Not this fucking shit you're bringing to me," Devil said. This man was the opposite of Tiny. He had a lot of prison years under his belt, and his club were into all kinds of dealings. Lash couldn't think of a single redeemable thing about the other club other than the fact they were loyal bastards. He'd rather be on Chaos Bleeds' good side than against them.

Over the years he'd heard how many men had lost their life by one of the club members. They were loyal, and betrayers were strung up and made to pay the piper as their statement was.

"One of my men has been taken. My daughter is in the hospital, and she almost lost my grandbaby. Eva, my woman, is hurting. I can't let this slide. I need you to help me, and we'll be indebted to you, I promise." Tiny was laying everything out on the table. The other club was not welcome to stay forever, but for the next couple of days they were welcome to the fold.

Lash watched as one of the men whispered in Devil's ear. The leader tensed up and nodded.

"We're always ready for a party, but we expect payment."

"I've got money," Tiny said.

"I don't need money. The boys and I have stopped travelling, and we've settled down in a place of our own." The other man dropped into a chair. Lash was surprised the wood didn't break under his weight. Devil was not fat, but he was a large fucker and dangerous. He put his weapon on the table and a load of hundred dollar bills. "I've got enough money to get anything I want. I'll help you kill these fuckers—and I mean dead in the ground— and you'll help me out with some information."

"What are you wanting?" Tiny asked.

"I'm looking for a girl, a whore. She shacked up with me over a year ago and disappeared."

Lash watched the proceedings knowing he'd have to wait to guarantee his brother's safety. He'd do anything for his brother, even listen to this fucker's love life.

"What's so important about the whore?" Tiny asked. There really was a difference in their world. Sweet-butts and whores were entirely different. Sweet-butts fucked bikers, and whores fucked anything for money.

"She took off pregnant with my kid. Don't give a fuck about the bitch, but I want my kid. She doesn't get fuck all from me."

"You're going to hurt her?" Tiny asked.

"I'm going to make sure everyone gets the message that they don't mess with me, Tiny. If you sent out a few more messages you wouldn't have bastards hurting your women and taking your men." Devil looked around the club. Angel was stood by his side, and Lash saw the other man's eyes land on her. He didn't like the interest in his eyes.

"Sweet-butt or old lady?" Devil asked.

"Pregnant old lady," Lash said, gritting his teeth to speak.

Devil smirked. "Get bored of him, sugar, and I'll take care of you."

Lash tightened his arm around his woman and glared at Tiny.

"Don't poach on my land, Devil."

"Look, I'll deal with my shit my way, and you deal with your shit your way. Do we have a deal?" Devil asked.

"Deal. Tell me the name of the woman," Tiny said.

"Karla Howard." The word was spat out of Devil's mouth. Lash knew the woman was as good as dead when the other man got to her. Whatever she'd done had put him on edge.

"Never heard of her," Tiny said.

"You got someone to find shit out? I've had no luck in that department."

"Whizz, run the name." Tiny didn't break eye contact as he let out the order. Whizz left the group and went to the nearest computer. "He'll have the answers you need."

"Good. Now tell me about the bastard who has your guys. No one touches a club bitch and gets away with it. Are they as sweet as that sugar there?" Devil asked.

Lash held her tighter, showing his claim. The sooner they found his brother and this club was on the road the happier he'd be.

****

Nash stared at his old supplier. The guy's bruises had all but disappeared from the last time he'd taken a swipe at the bastard. He shouldn't have let up at all. What was the guy's name? The men intent on giving him a headache left the room. Sophia was sobbing on the table.

"What's the matter, baby? We'll get out of this."

"Gill, the one who touched me, he and his goons were the ones who beat me up. If it wasn't for your brother I'd be in an awful state."

His grip on the chair tightened. He'd not known the connection the men had to his woman. Fuck, he needed to get them out of there.

"I'll protect you."

"He's your supplier, isn't he?" she asked.

"Yeah, I pissed him off."

She chuckled. "Do you really think we're getting out of here?" She wasn't fighting her cuffs, and he didn't like how desolate she looked.

"We're getting out of here. My brothers will be coming for both of us. They wouldn't leave us alone. I know they wouldn't," Nash said. He hoped to God they'd brought Chaos Bleeds. Before he'd been taken he didn't want them anywhere near Fort Wills, but now he saw the value in having the other biker club.

"Well, we're tired of all the sweetness going on in this room," Willy said, entering through the back of the warehouse door.

Nash stared at the older man, wishing he was free. He'd love to knock the smirk of the bastard's face. Willy wasn't even paying him any attention. The other man walked to Sophia's side.

"You really should have been nicer to me at work," Willy said, caressing her face. "This would have gone a lot differently."

She turned her head away from him.

Fight, Sophia. Don't let them win.

"Fuck off," Sophia said.

Willy laughed and slapped her around the face. She was already tender from the truck accident. Sophia cried out, whimpering.

The other two men walked into the room, Gill and Nash's supplier carrying their pouches with them. Whatever they had planned Nash knew he wasn't going to like it.

"So, we've been having a little talk with each other. Your supplier, we'll call him John seeing as you don't know his name, Nash, has given us a lot of information. You like your coke."

Gill lifted a white bag of powder.

"I'm over that shit," Nash said.

"We heard." Willy spoke up. "I've got a little problem, Nash. Someone hired me to get to you. The fact Sophia is part of the deal is just a bonus to me." Willy stroked a finger down her face. "I don't know what's going to happen to you, but I'm bored, and I like to hurt people."

Nash didn't like where this conversation was going. Who the fuck had hired Willy and Gill along with all those goons he'd seen? There was a lot more going on than he ever realized.

"So, we're thinking torture you and dope Sophia up," Gill said. "Our orders are to keep you alive and maybe weaken you a bit. They never said anything about hurting her."

"What the fuck is this about? Who the fuck hired you? Do you have any idea who you're fucking dealing with? She's innocent. What do you hope to achieve drugging her and beating the shit out of me?" Nash asked. He needed to protect Sophia. Getting her out of danger was his top priority, but he needed to know who wanted to keep him alive.

"Fort Wills is no longer going to belong to The Skulls. You and your men have overstayed their welcome. It's time fresh blood took over the town, and the men who hired us are the ones to do it."

Nash waited for more. "That it? Your diabolical plan is to get rid of The Skulls." Who would have hired these fucking thugs, and who wanted to take on The Skulls?

When they didn't say anything else, Nash started laughing. "You've got no fucking chance of getting rid of the club. We are the fucking town."

Gill walked over and slammed his fist into Nash's face. Sophia cried out. Staring up at the man who'd hurt his woman, Nash focused all his hatred toward the man in front of him. "We're going to get everything out of you, fucker. The Skulls will not know what hit them when one of their own gives them up. I believe your future and that of your club is going to be dead in the ground."

Again Nash laughed. "I'm not giving you anything."

"No?" Gill asked.

He stayed silent staring into the eyes of the man he was going to kill. Nash was going to tear Gill apart limb from limb, and he was going to enjoy it.

The other man turned to his ex-supplier who was holding a syringe. The guy arranged a tourniquet around her upper arm, finding a vein. The needle was pressed into Sophia's arm. Nash watched as his woman tensed. The drugs in the syringe were plunged into her body.

"A little heroin can go a long way," Gill said. "You start talking, or Sophia gets something else. I wonder how much shit she can take. Remember, Nash, our orders are only to keep you alive. We can find other whores to fuck. She was just a sweet deal."

Staring at his woman on the table Nash saw the high claiming her. The pain she'd been feeling moments ago was gone.

Fuck, fuck, fuck, fuck. Lash, I fucking need you right now.

He knew how powerful the drugs were. Sophia wouldn't survive the drugs. Heroin was fucking strong, which is why he never touched the shit. Fuck, he needed to get Sophia away from them. She was going to die if he didn't do something to stop them.

Gritting his teeth, Nash stared at the man in front of him. He knew his club well enough to know the men were doing everything they could to get to him. Stalling them could work, but he'd need to be careful or risk hurting Sophia more.

Think, idiot, think.

"So why am I supposed to give you this information? The Skulls are hard assed men. What do you have that we don't? Who wants me alive?" Nash asked.

He stared among all three men. Willy was looking at Sophia a little too intensely. Fuck, he hoped she wasn't allergic to any of the shit inside the drug. Today was supposed to be the best fucking day of his life, and at the moment it was turning into the fucking worst of his life.

Blowing out a breath he returned his focus back to Gill.

"Do you think we're that fucking stupid? We got a call. We answered it for a price. I will tell you something though. Every single one of us are all wanted for something."

"Petty thieves?" Nash asked.

Another punch landed to his jaw. When he was free he was cutting the guy's balls off and feeding them to him.

"Not even close," Gill said. "Murderers, rapists, and a couple of thieves added to the mix. We want a place to settle down, and Fort Wills is it for some of us."

"You think you're going to get the whole town to cooperate without ditching you fuckers to the nearest cop?" Nash asked. The Skulls succeeded because they helped the town. They were the law. These men were criminals to start off with. The town folk would turn on them in an instant once they learned the truth.

"Sophia's looking a little hot," Willy said, unbuttoning the front of the dress she was wearing. Staring over Gill's shoulder, Nash fought the restraints. He was so busy watching Sophia that he didn't see the knife pushed through his thigh until it was there.

He cried out from the instant hit of pain. Yeah, he was going to kill every single fucker in this room, and he was going to laugh while he did it.

"This is going to go easy or hard," Gill said. "It's up to you."

The dress was open to the waist. He was pleased Sophia had insisted on a bra. Every dirty, hurtful thing he could think of Nash was going to do to these men.

"She's not even fighting me," Willy said. "Maybe I should make him watch as I touch her?"

"Do what you want. Remember you promised me a turn, but don't fuck everything up. Scars wants everything clean for the pick up," Gill said.

"Stay the fuck away from her." Nash yelled the words spitting in Gill's face as he did. He earned another stab to the leg and punch across the face. With their attention focused on him they would leave his woman alone.

I'm so sorry, Sophia.

If he'd not gotten hooked on the drugs he wouldn't have put her in this position. He would do everything in his power to make it right.

No more drugs. No more fucking up.

"You're in no position to order anyone around." The man torturing him walked around him in a circle. Didn't these men know he'd been through hell and back? What they were throwing at him was nothing that The Skulls couldn't do.

He started laughing as he thought about the men, even the criminals outside, taking on the biker group. If Tiny had Chaos Bleeds with them, then these men would be screaming like girls within moments.

Another hit to the face didn't stop his laughter. Willy moved away from Sophia. Nash would keep them away from her.

"Stop hitting him, Gill. I want to know what he finds so amusing." Willy approached with his arms folded.

Hanging his head, Nash made sure the men were completely on him. Now all he needed to do was keep their attention and stall them. He didn't know how long he'd been at the warehouse, but the sun was already starting to set.

"Come on then, enlighten me," Willy said, bending forward.

Spitting out a mouthful of blood Nash looked up. "What I find so funny is you guys thinking you can win or even the bastards who hired thinking they could."

"We've got more than enough force to take you on." Willy no longer looked confident. The other man kept jerking his head in the direction of the door where their force was outside standing guard.

"You've got wanted men. Rapists, murderers, and a few fucking thieves to run the show. Whoever is in the background is fucking stupid. You're pawns in a bigger fucking game." Nash leaned his head back, looking up at the ceiling.

Talk slowly. Draw everything out.

Glancing past their shoulders he saw Sophia staring at him. Tears were streaming from her eyes.

"I love you." He watched her mouth the words to him.

173

Willy gripped his shoulders. "My men kill without thought."

"Your men were caught. The Skulls," Nash stopped to laugh, "they're murderers. My brother snapped a man's neck for touching his woman. You wouldn't last ten minutes with my brothers." They also had Killer along with plenty of other men. "We'd kill you all in a heartbeat."

The silence was deafening. Willy looked tense while Gill looked pale. His ex-supplier was gripping his bag of tricks like it was a lifeline.

"You said you had this in the bag. You said I'd be protected and that they guaranteed our protection," the supplier said.

"He's bluffing. They've got nothing. I've been promised, and no one crosses Scars or his club."
****

Sophia was conscious of the talk, but she felt the drugs in her system. They felt heavenly. There was not a single worry in her mind. When she turned her head and watched as Nash got hit, she knew the drugs were masking the pain.

Don't let them take over.

She'd heard that one hit of drugs could have you addicted. Lying on the table in danger of having far worse done to her, Sophia was determined not to get addicted to them. She'd enter any program they'd need to keep herself safe.

The guy who injected her started to move back. More shouting was happening.

"You're not going fucking anywhere. We're in this together," Gill said, pointing a bloody knife at each man.

I want to get out of here.

Prior to the drugs her mouth had felt awful and swollen. Now she couldn't feel anything or make any sense of her touch or taste. Licking her lips she stared up at the ceiling where there had been sunlight hours before. She no longer felt the pain of injuries, which she knew was bad for her.

Keeping her gaze on the ceiling she wondered how they were going to get out of this. If The Skulls didn't come then she knew she was in for a worse fate than being forced to take drugs. Her dress was half open, and the lust she'd seen in Willy's eyes couldn't be mistaken for anything else. She's also heard what Gill said. They were going to take it in turns to rape her.

Her body felt so light. Sophia tried to stay focused on that thought, but nothing was happening.

Willy moved beside her, reaching out to touch her. His hand hovered over her chest. She started laughing. Without the pain to immobilize her she could think of something else.

He gripped her face hard. "What the hell are you laughing about, whore?"

His hand was shaking where he held her in place.

"You're going to die. You're all going to die," she said, chuckling.

"That's my woman, men. She knows a lost cause when she sees one, and you guys are lost causes."

"You're fucking bluffing, and you know what, I'm going to fuck your whore right here," Willy said.

Sophia wriggled in the restraints wishing she could get free. Staring at the ceiling, she heard the sound of clothes being torn off.

Come on, someone save us. Please, please, please.

She begged and pleading, hoping and begging someone would save them.

Nash was screaming and cursing once again. The fear in his voice didn't help to settle her nerves. She didn't know how she'd be able to cope if Willy raped her.

"What the fuck are you doing?" the supplier asked. "This was not part of the fucking plan. I'm all for getting your rocks off, but this is not the fucking way to do it. Not with the deal you guys told me about. They should be here any minute."

For a split second Sophia liked him, but then she remembered what he'd done to her. The panic felt like it was in another part of her brain. She couldn't move, but she sensed her feelings rather than reacted to them. The fucker, she was so going to hurt him. How would he like it with his own drugs pushed through his fucking arm?

Her mind was all over the place. She couldn't deal with one solid form. Her dress was torn some more, and she screamed, wanting, no needing to get him as far away from her as possible.

"She's going to learn her place, and it's about time this fucker saw it," Willy said.

"No, you fuck her, and we're screwed. This is not part of the plan. There is a whole club looking for them. I'm not going to risk my life for this. She's yours once he's out of the equation and we're safely away from this fucking place." Whatever Nash had done to his supplier had put the fear inside him.

The supplier walked away toward the door. Gill looked ready to say something else.

Suddenly she turned her head as the sound of rumbling bikes filled the whole of the barn. She never thought the sound of bikes would comfort her. In those few moments it was the sound of heaven to her ears. Nash was smiling as he looked at the men.

"Showtime."

Chapter Thirteen

Nash was going to kiss every single bike he saw. Willy was pulling up his jeans as the sound of grunting met his ears. The front door to the warehouse was crashed through showing Lash holding a baseball bat. Men were everywhere with Gill, Willy, and the supplier charging out to fight.

Out of the corner of his eye he saw bikes with the emblem of the Chaos Bleeds. He owed Tiny a lot for bringing in the other biker club. Lash went to his side.

"Devil knew where you were. He asked about the surrounding area, and he came up with this. I couldn't even fucking think," Lash said.

"I don't give a fuck. You're here, and that's all that matters." The pain in his thigh was excruciating, and his body ached everywhere from the crash. Standing up was a chore, but he did it.

Lash helped him to his feet. The sounds of gunfire and screaming could be heard. He was so happy that the men had charged out of the warehouse to help their crew. Limping over to the table he pushed Sophia's dress together. He took the knife from Lash and tore at the rope holding her in place.

Cupping her cheek, he brushed his lips to hers.

"They injected her with heroin. I need you to stay with her, Lash." Nash stroked her cheek. "I love you, baby, but I'm going to go and hurt some men."

"Don't leave," she said.

"I'll carry her out, Nash. Don't worry about it. We've got more than enough men to cover the crew that contained you. They're not walking away alive." Lash wiped at his brow. "We rode hard and fast to get to you."

"I'm glad. I doubt they were going to wait around for something fun to do." Nash helped Sophia sit up. Her body was covered in a layer of sweat.

"I'll help her," Lash said. "Go."

He held her face between his hands. "The men that touched you, all of them, are going to die."

Lash took over, holding her steady as Nash walked out of the warehouse. He was limping even with his determination to see the end of the men who threatened his woman. Outside he saw several bodies on the ground. The three men he wanted were held captive by The Skulls. Chaos Bleeds were fighting some of the other men.

Nash didn't care about the others. There were three men he wanted to end. Behind him he heard Lash helping Sophia out of the building. The moment they were done he was taking her to the hospital. Zero was free and moved toward Sophia. Glancing behind him he saw Zero help her with her walking.

"Come on, we'll get her to a hospital," Zero said.

"No, I want to see," Sophia said, forcing both men to stop.

Tiny was holding Gill by the throat. "I got word there was an uprising in my town. I brought in recruits, and now it's time to show them what happens when they take on The Skulls."

Walking closer, Nash took the knife and gun Murphy and Butch handed him.

"These three were inside the barn. We saw them exit and figured our brother would like to hurt them."

Willy was whimpering, and the supplier was crying out, sobbing.

"This one has already pissed himself," Blaine said, holding Willy in place.

Nash stared at the three men feeling the anger build up inside him. He needed to end them, but before he did, he turned toward his woman.

The bruising was visible to him now as he looked at her. Dried blood coated her head, and there were marks along her arm. She was holding her dress together. Sophia shivered. Her black hair fell around her in waves. She looked like an angel sent from hell.

"Kill them, Nash. They were going to torture us." She stopped, licking her split lip. "And they were going to do far more than that with me. I need to see them dead instead of looking over my shoulder."

Staring into her eyes, Nash saw the truth in her eyes. The men before him had to die before she could feel safe once again.

Turning back to the men, he pointed at Gill. "You, I'm hurting you last."

He moved toward the supplier. Bending down, he picked out three syringes and headed toward the men.

Supplier started screaming and fighting the hold his brothers had on him. "You injected my woman and were happy to do so." Sticking in the syringes, Nash stared into his eyes as he plunged the shit into his body. "Let's see how you like it."

Nash didn't stop injecting the man until he had no pulse. There was no satisfaction inside him. He checked to make sure Sophia was handling what she was seeing. When he didn't see revulsion in her eyes, he moved on to Willy.

He felt the respect and love of his club behind him. They had his back, and now he was able to prove to them all that he was never going to go off the rails again. When Willy stopped screaming and finally ceased to live, he turned all of his hatred onto Gill. This fucker was going to get the worst kind of treatment.

****

Snitch felt his anger turn to rage as he saw the beginning of his plan crumble around him. Tiny was with Devil from Chaos Bleeds. If the other biker group had been picked it wouldn't have fucking mattered. He would have gotten what he wanted most, revenge against Tiny, the leader of the fucking Skulls.

"We've got to get out of here, boss," Scars said.

"You fucked this up. You promised me these men would do the job. They left his brother alive, and they're being killed." Snitch grabbed the handlebars of his bike tightly.

"I gave the orders, and they fucked them up." Scars argued his point. "We've got to come up with another plan. If we don't get out of here we're going to be on their list of fuckers to kill."

Snitch kept his gaze on the scene at the warehouse. They'd been minutes late from getting Nash. All he'd wanted was for Nash to be alive. With the biker alive, and being both weak and close to Tiny, he'd have gotten information out of the bastard before killing him. Taking The Skulls down one by one had been a good plan. Settling his gaze on Tiny, he knew he'd have to be patient to get to the man he wanted. He was going to kill Tiny, claim the town, and finally have his revenge.

Wait, plan, and succeed.

"Sleep well, Tiny. You're not going to be sleeping for long." Gunning his bike, he pulled away without being seen.

****

Sophia lay in the hospital bed hearing the nurses and doctors around the room. Nash was in the emergency room being treated for his injuries whereas she was laid out on the bed waiting for the heroin to leave her system. When the doctor said she could be clear of the drugs, she'd never felt so happy in all of her life. The problem would come after the drugs were out of her system. They were keeping her in to monitor her reaction afterwards. She'd been terrified by the consequences of the drugs inside her and knowing they could still have an effect, terrified her more. All she could do was wait.

She was also in the bed for a concussion and several cracked ribs. The crash in the truck had caused her far more damage than the drugs. The doctor hadn't liked the damage he'd seen and sent her for x-rays along with blood tests. Staring at the blank white wall, Sophia wished someone would give her an update on what was happening.

A feminine voice cleared its throat. Looking up, Sophia saw Tate sat in a wheelchair in the doorway. The other woman was wearing a hospital gown.

"Murphy told me what happened. He's gone to get an update, and I thought I'd check on you." Tate wheeled into the hospital room.

"Are you all right?"

"Considering I was run down by a maniac, I'm all right," Tate said, stroking her stomach. "I'm relieved. My little baby is doing okay. How are you?"

"I'm handling it." Sophia sat up, reaching out to take her hand.

"They're keeping me for observation." Tate tightened her hold.

"I'm sorry about everything that has happened to you."

Tears welled in Tate's eyes. "It's a risk you take by being with them. Murphy can't stand the idea of anything bad happening to me. He's just going to have to get used to the fact I'm not going anywhere. I love him, and I'm not leaving him. I'm his old lady, but he's my old man."

She listened to Tate talk. It was nice listening to another woman talk for a change. She'd been alone with bikers for such a long time she'd started to forget what female company felt like.

"Are you going to tell me what went down tonight?"

Sophia bit her lip. Watching Nash kill all three men hadn't bothered her, and she didn't know if that was what upset her or not. She told Tate everything how he killed the drug dealer with his own drugs and cut off Willy's dick and fed it to him. With Gill, he smashed his face in. She wasn't afraid of Nash. He'd protected her when she needed it. Her love was not wavering. She still wanted to be in his life without any worry.

Murphy cleared his throat alerting them to his presence. "Nash is causing a fuss wanting to see you. The doctors and nurses won't let him here until he takes their tests. He was in the accident as well." He handed Tate some tea.

She watched Murphy stroke Tate's cheek and then caress her shoulder. "How are you feeling?" he asked.

"I'm good, baby. Nothing is going to keep me down. I'm here for the long run. I've got a feeling little baby bump is, too." Tate covered his hand, smiling.

"We'll get through this."

"When you see Nash, tell him I'm waiting for him when he can come up," Sophia said. Murphy nodded, and after ten minutes he pulled Tate from the room, moving her away. She watched the other woman go.

Alone once again, she lay back waiting for her man to come. The sound of another man clearing his throat alerted her to being watched. She glanced at the door to see Zero leaning against the doorframe.

"Nash is on his way. He got the all clear, and he's signing all the paperwork for you both," Zero said.

She nodded. "Thank you for taking care of me," she said.

"I'll always take care of you." He entered the room, going to the chair beside her bed and taking hold of her hand. "You'll be part of our family soon, and I'll do everything in my power to protect you."

"I really do appreciate it." His hand was warm, and she noticed how he stroked her wrist. Zero ran his thumb over the pulse in her wrist.

"The thought of anything happening to you makes me feel sick."

His honesty was scaring her.

"Zero, I'm with Nash."

He stopped her talking with putting a hand in the air. "Please let me finish."

"I know you have feelings for me. The way you are around me is different from the other women. I saw it that day you were testing Nash. You didn't treat any of the other women differently." She couldn't keep her thoughts locked up inside when she knew the truth.

She looked up as he sat down, resting his hand on his thigh.

"Yes, I have feelings for you. I don't know how deeply or how they came about. All I know is that when it comes to you, I'll always have your back. I won't let Nash hurt you."

Tears filled her eyes. She didn't feel anything for this man other than friendship.

"I can't give you anything," she said.

"I know. For the first time in my life I'm not asking you for anything." He leaned down, pressing his lips to hers. "That is all I'm going to take from you."

He got up and started to leave the room. "Don't worry about anything, Sophia. The Skulls will always have your back. You'll never be alone again."

She watched him go. Lying back against her bed she let out a sigh. Her thoughts were set on Nash. Maybe if she'd met Zero first there could have been a chance, but she doubted it. Zero didn't make her heart race. She never searched for him in a room. Nash called to her in ways she didn't understand. Her love for him had been part of her for so long that she didn't want to give him up.
****

Nash was stood outside of Sophia's door waiting for Zero to exit. No one inside the room could see him as he was stood a little out of the way. Checking out the time, he waited, giving Zero the chance to get his thoughts off his chest.

When the other brother stepped outside of the room, Nash saw he paused when he saw him.

"Nash," Zero said.

Folding his arms over his chest, Nash stared at his fellow brother and Skull. "Are we going to have a problem?" Nash asked.

"The only problem we'll have is if you treat that woman in any other way than if she's a princess." Zero took several steps away. "I'll never hurt you or her. I just needed to get it off my chest." The other man shrugged. "She's in love with you."

"I'll never hurt her, Zero. Sophia is the love of my life."

Nash saw the smile on Zero's face.

"Then we'll be good. I'll see you tomorrow." Nash was slapped on the back, and then Zero turned away and left.

Frowning, Nash shook his head. He wouldn't get into it with Zero.

Going to the door he saw Sophia was lying in bed staring at the ceiling.

"Hey, baby," he said.

Her face lit up. "I was wondering when you were going to get here."

"All the club is here. Tiny is keeping an eye on Tate and Eva."

"How is Eva?"

"She's out of the coma, and we're hoping she'll be good to go home soon. All the boys are tired of ending up in the hospital. Our women should be protected at all times." He closed the door and moved to the bed. Nash didn't sit down. He lay down beside her, getting Sophia to curl up against him.

"If a nurse catches you she's going to go mad," she said.

"Don't give a fuck. I couldn't hold you today, and I need to be able to hold you."

The club wasn't going back to the clubhouse. Whizz was sorting out the business for Devil. Lash had caught him up to speed on everything he missed.

"I know this is probably the worst time to ask, but will you marry me?" Nash asked.

She looked up at him. "Yes, I'll marry you."

"The drugs are out of my life, baby. I'm not having anything to do with them. I'll fight it every step of the way. If something comes of what happened to you today, I'll be with you. You're not getting rid of me."

Sophia pressed a finger to his lips.

"I love you. There's nothing to dispute. I'll marry you. Now shut the fuck up and hug me."

She settled closer to him. He held her tightly, closing his eyes and knowing they were only ever going to grow closer from that day forward.

Kissing the top of her head, he closed his eyes. The last twenty-hour hours had been a nightmare. He couldn't imagine going through anything like that and coming out the other end stronger. Sophia made him stronger by sticking beside him.

Sleep claimed him, and even the nurse couldn't force him to move when he woke up.

Chapter Fourteen

The rumor around town about what went down at the warehouse was a drug bust gone bad. Nash thought it was rather inventive of the people even though everyone knew the truth. The club and Chaos Bleeds had dealt with the bodies burying them all. Whizz found out that all of the men were wanted criminals, even Willy. What they hadn't found out was who had hired them. He didn't feel any guilt over killing the men. Nash would do it again in a heartbeat in order to protect his woman.

Within a month the club was back to normal. Sophia didn't have any lasting effects of the heroin in her system, which was a fucking relief. Eva was healthy once again even if she did look a little pale and never left without a prospect. Nash knew the prospect was down to Tiny. His leader couldn't stand for Eva to be alone. Tate was also back to being her bossy self. There was a nervousness to her eyes that Nash hoped would fade with time and with the advancing months of her pregnancy. He made sure to be patient around her at all times. Of course, Tate knew what was happening and made it hard for him to want to be nice to her.

Kelsey was having a hard time with Killer. The dental nurse wouldn't visit Killer. Kelsey spoke with the women, and Nash even saw her hanging out at the salon with them, but she wouldn't give Killer the time of day.

Out of his drug haze, Nash was able to properly mourn the death of Mikey and even took flowers to Kate's graveside with Sophia. Together they said goodbye to her sister. He'd not been tempted by drugs, and he wouldn't touch drink either. When the parties were in full swing, he settled for a soda or water. He wasn't prepared to fall off the wagon.

Sophia stayed with him and even started going back to college. After three weeks of looking they'd found a house near his brother's. They had put down a deposit and were moving in within the next week. His brothers were helping with the move. Zero helped the most and spent a lot of time with Sophia. The friendship between his woman and Zero was confusing but it worked, and he wasn't going to take something like that away from them. Nash couldn't stop the guy's feelings. He just hoped Zero wasn't stupid enough to act on them.

After everything that happened, Chaos Bleeds stayed in town for some time, celebrating their kills. Nash actually enjoyed their company. Devil was one mean son of a bitch. He didn't know how Devil and Tiny were friends, but everyone could see a bond between the two men. They'd clearly been through a lot together.

The other biker group only left when Whizz coughed up some information. Kayla had a sister by the name of Lexie. They gave him the town and an address for the woman. With that tucked away in his pocket, Devil rode out, taking all of his group with him.

Sitting on the edge of his bed, Nash looked up to see Sophia walking out of the bathroom. She wore a denim skirt that ended at her knee and one of his rock shirts. His cock thickened, and he wanted to throw her to the bed and fuck her senseless.

"What are you doing?" she asked, looking at his notebook then back at him.

"I'm doing some rough calculations for the work we want doing. The guys have agreed to help with the building." He tapped his pencil on the book. Working on the house took his mind off other worries like the fact she still hadn't had her monthly cycle. All the time they'd been together, she hadn't stopped him at all.

She walked over, pressing her hand to the page. "Stop worrying about the expense. I don't need everything done immediately. I like to take my time with projects. Everything is going to be fine."

Dropping the book to the floor, he reached out, sinking his fingers into her hair and drawing her close. "Then kiss me, baby."

He swallowed down her moan as his other hand ran his fingers up the inside of her thigh. Nash couldn't keep his hands off her. All he ever wanted to do was fuck her and fuck her hard.

"Stop screwing around, you two. It's time for your send off party," Lash said, kicking the door as he passed.

Sophia giggled, dropping her head to his chest. Chuckling, Nash stroked the curls off her face. "We better go and face the music. Tiny's going to kick our ass out of the room."

"Come on. It's time for us to go," she said, taking hold of his hand. "I'm ready for a send off."

They exited the bedroom together, and as they hit the stairs the room erupted in applause. Nash smiled, enjoying the whistles and catcalls coming their way. Sophia was one of them now, and the club had accepted her as part of their family. He couldn't have asked for anything more.

She hadn't married him yet. Tate was organizing a wedding for Christmas. He didn't care as long as his name was on a piece of paper signaling their marriage.

Tiny and Eva was stood side by side watching them.

"Tonight we're celebrating the end of our enemies and the start of new beginnings," Tiny said, raising his glass.

Nash was handed a soda, and he noticed Sophia had the same.

"The last couple of months, in fact the last few years, have been rocky for all of us." Tiny turned to Angel and Lash. "We're all stronger for having a woman prepared to take the risks." He moved to Tate and Murphy. "We've lost something we can never get back, and I know Mikey would have had so much to say. Beside all of the shit, we're being given a chance to keep living, to keep moving and to bring the future Skulls into the fold."

The emotion was welling up inside Nash.

"So I propose a toast to Angel and Lash for their unborn child and to the child they lost. You guys deserve so much happiness, and I know it's going to be one spoiled brat. To Tate and Murphy, we'll never forget what you could have lost, and we'll embrace what comes of the future. And to my grandbaby. To Nash, you fucked up, man, but that's all in the past. I'm lucky to have you on my team. Sophia, you brought him back and make him a better man. The Skulls will protect you for the rest of your life." Tiny's glass rose in the air. "To new beginnings, bad endings, and a future filled with promise."

Sipping at the soda Nash wrapped his arm around Sophia's shoulders. Sandy was stood beside the music box. The good doctor had finally made it through even though it had been touch and go.

"Let's make some noise." The music was turned up to blasting. Sandy climbed on the table followed by several sweet-butts, Rose, and Tate. The dancing was not rushed or a riot. The women who'd been hurt took it steady. Nash saw Tate being careful as she moved. Murphy was right there, supporting her.

He heard Sophia giggling at their dancing. She put the glass down, wrapping her arms around his shoulders.

"Nah, you've not got a chance," Tate said, reaching down to grab Sophia's hand. His woman didn't let Tate hurt herself. "It's time for a dance. Angel, you may be preggers, but get your ass up here. Hold on, I'm preggers, too. Fuck, we've got to celebrate. "

Nash stood back as he watched his woman surrounded by her friends. He was so fucking lucky to call her his woman.

Sipping at his soda he watched her having the time of her life. He wouldn't spoil this for her.

Lash stood beside him. "Watching my woman dance is one of my favorite things to do."

He understood why. Watching Sophia swing her hips from side to side to the music turned him the fuck on. The moment he got her to their home, he was having her ass. All of their worries were behind them. In no time at all they'd be married.

After four hours of watching her dance and sing with the other old ladies and sweet-butts, Nash lost his patience. He picked her up and carried her outside to the car. His bike was in desperate need of some repairs.

In between working on the house he was also working on his bike.

"We were having fun," Sophia said, pouting.

"We're about to have more fun."

He broke the speed limit getting her to their house. Parking the car, he walked around to her side of the door. Lifting her up in his arms, he cupped her ass as she wrapped her legs around his waist. Her giggle was driving him crazy.

"I can feel your cock, Nash. You've got some kinky shit planned for me today, don't you?" she asked.

Grunting, he searched for the key and opened the door after several attempts. Not watching where he was going, he slammed the door shut and went straight for the stairs. Tate had told him she'd kitted the bedroom out. They had enough furniture to get them by.

Dropping her to the bed, he tore at his clothes and then reached for her. He got her naked within minutes. Opening her thighs, he dragged her to the edge of the bed. He exposed her swollen clit and took her into his mouth, sucking on her nub.

She cried out, thrusting up to meet him. Sophia was soaking already, and he swallowed down every drop. With his fingers he coated her anus, getting her slick.

Once she climaxed the first time, exploding on his tongue, Nash took a step away. He went to the drawers and pulled out the tube of lube he owned. Coating his shaft with a great deal of lube, he went back to the bed.

There was no need for words. He was so fucking in love with her, and all he wanted to do was drown in her scent. Gripping her hips he pulled her to her knees. Her anus glinted at him in the half light.

He couldn't wait to be inside her.

****

Sophia was so turned on she couldn't wait for him to fuck her. Over the last couple of weeks he'd been teasing her ass and driving her wild with the thought of him taking her ass. Glancing behind her, she smiled at him. He was working his shaft, fisting the length. His gaze was on her ass.

"Do you want me, baby?" Nash asked.

"Yes. Fuck me, Nash."

He slapped her ass making her yelp. She held her breath as he grabbed her hip, and then the tip pressed against her anus. Gasping, she tensed up waiting for the pain.

"Don't tense up. Remember how my fingers feel."

Closing her eyes, she rested her head on the bed and breathed out, finally relaxing. He pushed the tip of his cock inside her, going past the tight ring of muscles until the head of his shaft was inside her. The burn shocked her, but the pleasure did not. She loved the burn with the slight edge of pain to her pleasure.

"So fucking beautiful. I can see your ass opening up taking my cock."

Groaning, she felt an answering pulse deep inside her pussy.

"Touch yourself. I want you to explode with pleasure."

She did as he asked stroking her clit. Her orgasm was so close to the surface, and she felt Nash go deeper inside her ass. He took his time with his thrusts, going shallow at first.

"I want to feel you come before I fuck you completely."

Working her clit, she stroked herself while feeling him caress her back and ass. His cock pulsed like a hot brand inside her ass.

Her pussy was wet, and she didn't need any lube to stroke herself.

Moaning, she closed her eyes and allowed herself to open up under his assault. Crying out, she whimpered as her orgasm took over, slamming inside her.

He pulled out of her mid-way through her first orgasm. "Fuck, you're going to have to get used to me taking your ass, baby."

Nash gripped her hips and rode her hard. There was no pain, only the slight edge that came with the pleasure.

She held onto the bed as he reached around bringing her to another orgasm as he fucked her.

Sophia couldn't make any sense of what was happening. Nash was entirely in control of everything they were doing. She couldn't think straight or understand what was going on.

The pleasure was at an all time peak, and there was no way to stop it. Crying out, she slammed back against him needing him to make it burn.

When he slapped her ass, she cried out wanting more from him. His thrusting increased, and so did his strokes to her clit.

They charged toward the peak together until finally she went hurtling over the edge. She felt him tense inside her ass and the heat as he released. Collapsing to the bed, she took several deep breaths in an attempt to calm down her nerves.

She was shaking all over. Nash locked their fingers, his body curved behind her back. "You're so fucking sexy. I'm the luckiest man in the world," he said, whispering against her ear. He kissed her cheek then her neck. Her nipples tightened, and she wanted to go again.

"That was amazing," she said.

"It's not going to be our last. We're going to do it again and again."

Closing her eyes, she moaned. "I don't think I can handle another round just yet. I'm getting old."

He chuckled. "We'll build up your stamina. You'll be wanting it all the time."

"I do want it all the time. I'm going to struggle when I go back to classes next month." She'd signed up for her course. Her teachers demanded she do several course papers and pass an exam before she was allowed to go back on the course. They wanted to make sure she was dedicated and wouldn't quit on them.

She'd completed everything apart from the exam. There was a problem, and she really needed to tell Nash. He was going to be wondering why she was getting fat and refusing to go to class.

"God, I love you. I can't wait to be married to you."

"What about a baby?" she asked, chancing a look at him.

"A baby?"

"Yeah, I hope a baby is in your future. I did a test, and it was positive. We're going to have a little boy or girl." She spoke fast so he wouldn't drag the revelation out.

"Pregnant. You're pregnant?"

She nodded. "I need to book an appointment, but then I thought I'd find out who Angel is seeing and go to him or her." Sophia was cut off as Nash slammed his lips down on hers.

"You know how to take a guy by surprise."

"Are you happy?"

"I'm fucking ecstatic. I can't wait to tell the guys. This is going to be fucking good for my ego." He turned her face toward him, kissing her lips.

"Are you sure about this?" she asked. "A kid is a big deal."

"That kid is our big deal, and I couldn't think of any better way of living my life than with a kid."

Her fears melted away as he kissed her deeply. "We need to shower and get washed. I'm fucking your pussy tonight."

Nash was never going to win an award for being a romantic, but Sophia loved him, and there was nothing she wouldn't do for him. Being an old lady certainly had its perks.

She giggled as he picked her up heading toward the bathroom. He was singing, and the smile on his face would stay with her forever.

NASH

Epilogue

Tiny watched as the prospect he'd assigned to take Eva home walked away from the house. The guy was given the security code to lock the gate behind him. He wouldn't put her life at risk anymore. Out of all the women Eva always seemed to be the one who ended up in most danger, and he wasn't having it anymore. Especially not with the history his club had, and not only his club but him as well.

They were not arguing, which he considered a good thing. She wasn't giving him anything. Since their time in Vegas Eva hadn't given him the time of day. The night she'd gotten drunk she'd forced him to relook a lot of things. She hated their time together and didn't want anything from him other than a friendship.

He was trying, but in his mind and heart Eva was his woman.

Opening the door to his home, he made his way silently up to her room. He found her sat at her desk removing her jewelry and brushing out her hair. She was so beautiful. Her eyes were dark brown along with her hair, but there was something about her that drew her in. "The prospect only just left. Did you leave your party to follow me?" she asked, looking at him through their reflections.

"You left without saying goodbye."

"I rarely stick around for your parties. I've only been invited to a few, and I wasn't there for any reason other than the fact the prospect needed to be there," she said. She put the brush down and turned to him.

"The clubhouse is for you, Eva."

"You screw your women there, Tiny. I've heard them all talking about your prowess in the bedroom. You're a monster, a machine in the sack. This life is not for me.

Tate is grown up. Lash and Nash are back on track. You don't need me anymore."

Stepping closer, he sank his fingers into her hair. "I don't need you?"

"You've never needed me."

He slammed his lips down on hers, tasting the vanilla on her tongue from the flavor tea she loved so much. Tiny had banned her from drinking after her outburst. He'd been surprised when she agreed to it.

Seeing Devil had reminded him a lot about his past. The men he'd left behind in his search for perfection. The past always had a way of catching up when you least expected it. In his gut, Tiny had a feeling his was about to catch up with him. When it came to Eva he'd been running from what she made him feel. Even Alex, Patricia's brother, had told him to start moving on. Patricia was dead and was never coming back.

What he once felt for Patricia didn't even begin to cover what he felt for Eva. The woman before him had worked her way under his skin, and there was no getting away from it. Eva was in his blood.

His dick thickened, needing inside her.

She pulled away from him. Her hands were on his arms, holding him off. "Stop this, Tiny. I'm not your dead wife, and I'm never going to be."

He'd brought her up time and time again. It had been years, but Tiny didn't feel anything for Patricia anymore. That part of his life was gone, and like Devil he was going to start taking what he wanted.

"This is not about her. This is about us." He tugged her close, stroking a hand down to her breast. "And we're going to do this, Eva. You're going to be my old lady."

She snorted. "It's not going to last for long."

"Why not?" he asked, fully intending to keep her by his side even if he had to bind her there with fucking handcuffs.

"My father is coming to get me. I'm leaving Fort Wills for good. I'm going back to Vegas."

Over his dead fucking body!

The End

www.samcrescent.wordpress.com

Evernight Publishing

www.evernightpublishing.com

Made in the USA
Charleston, SC
03 May 2015